EMMA LOUISE HAMBLING

Who Did It
in the
Cotswolds?

Jamieson Hart, Fund Manager and

Coincidental Detective Series

All characters and events in this publication, other than those clearly in the public domain, are fictitious and any resemblance to real persons, living or dead, is purely coincidental. All opinions expressed are not necessarily those of the author.

ISBN-13: 978-0-6480330-5-9
ISBN-10: 0-6480330-5-8

Other books in the Jamieson Hart series:

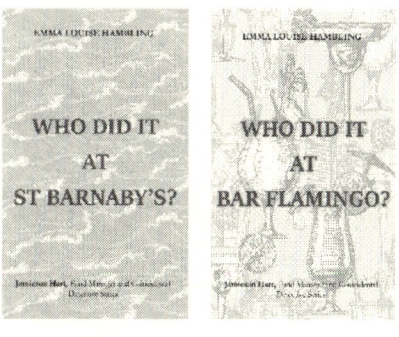

To Dennison, Douglas, Edward and Sadie

Characters

Jamieson Hart – partner at Glasward-Sade Hart

Amelia Hart – ex-wife and author

Mirabelle – Jamieson's Chilean housekeeper

Fraser Jones – friend and detective

Sam – friend, married to **Tilda**

Clarence – married to **Juliette,** they own The Pied Piper

Samrina – management consultant, married to Sanjay

Sanjay – lecturer in religion, married to Samrina

Donald Crabshaw – hedge fund manager

Polly – lust interest and barrister

Jordan Sticks – professional soccer player

Norrie – Tilda's uncle

Veda and Barbara – Tilda's aunts

Sandra – business partner in Singapore office

Penelope – work sidekick in Singapore office

Sinclair – Goldman Sachs sharebroker

Kenneth Chow – Singaporean billionaire

Wes – CEO of Xtrapak

Brie – casual lust interest

Chapter 1

'Jamieson, Jamieson! Open the bloody door! Aargh, this is one of the many reasons why we got divorced – you are so slow. Come on! I know you're in there!'

I somewhat undelightedly pulled open the solid wood hotel-suite door. Amelia, my stunning but slightly irritating ex-wife with impeccably bad timing, toppled through the frame. 'Hi, about time – a turtle could move faster than you. Where's the toilet? I'm desperate and my room won't be ready for an hour.'

'Through there,' I pointed. 'Why didn't you use the hotel's facilities?'

'You know I don't like using public toilets – disgusting. Who knows what you might catch from a loo seat?' As Amelia shut the bathroom door behind her, my brain went into overdrive. The shit was about to hit the fan.

'Jamieson, whose shoes are these?' Amelia exited, holding a pair of particularly high silver, strappy heels.

'A past guest left them behind, maybe?'

'And you haven't yet taken them to reception? Unlikely. Have you got company?'

'Yes, he has, actually. Who are you?'

The shit had hit the fan and was about to spin into overdrive.

'I am Amelia, Jamieson's ex-wife. Who are you?'

'Someone who doesn't go banging on other people's doors demanding to be let in when they have no right.'

'Is that so? How old are you? About twenty-five? Shall we sit down, sweetie, and I can tell you a bit about life and relationships and how they work, so when you're Jamieson's age – which I estimate will be in about seventy-five years' time – you might be a little wiser in your decision making.'

I hate it when Amelia's right – and knowing full well that Brie would not be able to match her in the verbal boxing ring, I interjected, 'Brie, maybe it's time you left.'

'Me go? We were just getting started, until that cow thumped on the door like an over-sized elephant and you threw a duvet over me. I do have some self-respect, you know.'

'Sleeping with a man twice your age? I doubt it, honey. And don't use two different animals as metaphors in the same sentence – it sounds weird.'

'Amelia, stop. Sorry, Brie, unfortunately my ex-wife may have helped me see light of day and I hate to admit it but I may be too old for you.'

'You reckon?' Amelia rolled her eyes.

Brie responded, 'I can see why you're no longer with her. Fine. Your loss. You will have to imagine what I was about to do to you because you will never get to experience the pleasure.'

I closed the door behind Brie and turned to Amelia, who'd taken a seat on the sofa and was showing interest in one of the magazines spread on the coffee table. I adored this woman but she drove me crazy in equal measure. For some reason, unknown to any kind of rationality, this run-in she'd had with my latest lust interest had turned me on and I was desperate to take her to the boudoir and show her how I felt. I knew my chances of being successful in that quest were up there with snow on a summer's day so I slumped into an armchair, put my feet on the table and waited for the barrage.

'So, fancy yourself as a sugar-daddy, do you?'

'Oh, please.'

'She was a twenty-something-year-old girl. And it's three in the afternoon! You think she chose a guy in his forties for any reason other than money?'

'I think my obvious intelligence, good humour, and biceps won her over.'

'You are impossible.'

'But you like that about me.'

'Aargh, you drive me insane!'

'Okay, let's forget this unpleasant encounter, and talk about the kids. Were they okay with your folks moving in to look after them when you left?'

'I'm too tired to argue with your topic change. Yes, they were fine – thankfully they weren't here to witness their dad with a slut, blemishing the character of this particularly charming bed and breakfast.'

'Pump the brakes, would you?'

'Okay. I must say though, this jet-lag's hit me hard, I've no idea where in the world I am. All I know is that I arrived at Heathrow around lunchtime then got driven here, the most perfect little village I could ever imagine existed. We had to wait for a farmer to move his sheep across the one-car-wide lane on the way in here, and at the final bridge a mother duck stopped us in her tracks when she decided her ducklings needed to cross the road. I can't believe all the houses are built of thick stone, with thatched rooves, and the place is actually called Avon-On-The-Water. I don't know whether I've gone back in time a thousand years or fallen into a pretty jigsaw puzzle. Oh, gosh, I need some sleep.' With that, Amelia closed her blue eyes and put her head (covered with long brunette hair) on the edge of the sofa. She was exquisite.

My name is Jamieson Hart and I am a partner at the firm Glasward-Sade Hart in Singapore, but I choose to work from home in South Beach. This set-up gives me distance from all the 'noise' generated by suits in Singapore, enabling me to make winning investment decisions, and be recognised, consistently, as one of the world's top performing fund managers.

My bachelor pad in South Beach is situated right next door to Amelia and my three children. I will love Amelia for the rest of my life but for now we are better apart – that's what she says anyway.

Amelia and I are here in this village in the Cotswolds to celebrate my long-time friend Sam and his wife's renewal of marriage vows. England is a far distance from home but Tilda is British and wanted to return to her roots for the occasion.

My other friend, Fraser, is also in the Cotswolds with us. The whole 'renewal of vows' thing came about during a unique ski trip in which Sam, Fraser and I ended up trapped in a hotel fearing for our lives. Sam had done some soul searching during this time and realised he had taken Tilda for granted – so here we were, ready to witness 'a rejuvenation of their love' as the invitation had stated.

Holidays don't exist in my line of business; however, I was looking forward to some relaxation and fresh, country air. Unfortunately, the peace was to be disturbed by former work foes and murder.

Chapter 2

Magnesium salts had been supplied by The Pied Piper (the name of the boutique hotel and pub or, as some people call it, bed and breakfast) so I took to the bath, leaving Amelia crashed out on the sofa. I had been mulling over an investment opportunity and used the time to help clarify my thoughts.

I am forced for PR reasons to have a team, although I far prefer to work on my own. My side-kick, Penelope, likes to bore me with her investment ideas – contrary to what every great investor would do, she panics at the sign of a sharemarket downturn and wants to cash up all our investments. On the other hand, when the market is facing a cyclical peak, she gets caught up in the heady rush and finds numerous 'fantastic buying opportunities'. I don't know why she hasn't learnt yet that market downturns throw up buying opportunities and that investing in a bubble is not a wise move. Still I keep her on since she manages a lot of the day to day reports that I simply have no time or inclination to endure.

Sandra, my partner at the firm, is a total contrast. She is sharp. It is her dedication and determination that has largely built the firm to where it is today. She's also a master at convincing prospective clients to sign with the firm. Her ability to understand the world of investing and close sales, coupled with my performance track record, makes us a formidable team.

The prospect that had caught my eye lately was an Australian-based manufacturing firm named Xtrapak that produced all kinds of packaging – boxes, wraps, bags, cartons and containers – for a variety of industries. It had a significant number of assets globally and minimal levels of debt, and its sheer size should have enabled it to attain large economies of scale and price smaller competitors out of the market. The problem was that Xtrapak's CEO was a boffin. A boffin supported by a board of monkeys.

This poor management, combined with unreliable distribution times, meant the business was struggling to cover costs. The CEO, Wes, was looking to raise funds, and I was interested – largely in what I could do with the firm if I were able to take control. There was an opportunity to be had here; I just had to put all the pieces together.

For fear of actually turning into a prune, I exited the bath and wrapped my lower half in one of the over-sized, soft towels. Amelia stirred on the sofa and my imagination danced as I saw her skirt had bunched a little too far up her legs.

'Oh, my goodness.' She yawned. 'I didn't want to have a snooze. I wanted to push through till tonight, get a good sleep then start the day fresh tomorrow – it's the only way to force myself out of this ten-hour time shift.'

She stretched and pushed her skirt back to its decent place. 'Do you feel like going for a walk around the village before dinner? I think some cool evening air would do me good. And I need to get out of here because you're looking a bit too hot with no top on. I don't want to do something I'll regret.'

Amelia was flirting with me, wasn't she? 'Come on, there would be no regrets.'

'Yes, there would. How about you put some clothes on and we head out.'

Even though it was early summer, the evening air was cool, about ten degrees Celsius, so I put on a pair of jeans, a long-sleeved, blue-checked shirt and a beige jacket.

After walking down the narrow lane from The Pied Piper, we reached the village of Avon-On-The-Water which had one main road winding through the middle of a mix of cottages and shops. Well, at a stretch it could be called a road – I counted two moving cars in ten minutes. I had been told that since the sun was about to set, the day-tripping tourists would likely have left to join the hordes on the M40 London bound.

I spotted a sign saying *Bert's Coffee House*. I had a feeling Bert and I were going to be seeing a lot of each other since The Pied Piper's coffee machine was out-of-action. Amelia chose to stay on the street, taking photos, while I wandered inside to be greeted by a short, overweight man with curly hair on half his head below a top of baldness.

'Come in, if you must. I was just closing up but I can delay going home to meet your requirements.'

Hmm, it seemed Bert was a bit frazzled, to be generous. 'I was just after a mochaccino, thanks – a caffeine shot to get me though the evening.'

'A mochaccino, no problem.' With that he assembled what I'm sure was his answer to latte, mochaccino, flat white, macchiato and any other city slicker's request. He shoved a bowl of hardened sugar cubes across the counter. 'Four quid.'

I forked some change from my pocket. 'Tough day?'

'No different to any other. Too many bloody tourists.'

I was getting a different feeling about Avon-On-The-Water than Amelia, snapping away outside with her camera.

'They don't appreciate the burden they place on the locals?' I cautiously asked.

'It's mainly the London toffs I have a problem with. Swoop in for the day in their Lamborghinis, Porsches and four-wheel drive Audis, take up all the parking spaces, pollute the air, talk to me like I'm a piece of dirt, mess up my place, then accelerate out of here near-missing the sheep and ducks and other creatures that call this place home. I assumed you were one of them till I heard you speak.'

'No, not from London, and no car. I'm dependent on my legs this holiday.'

'Are you staying at The Pied?'

'Yes, here for some friends who are renewing their vows.'

'Bloody heck, who would want to go through their wedding day twice? Enough stress on the one day to last a lifetime, I say. My Mrs wouldn't talk about anything else for months before we tied the knot. Darn right annoying. Missed out on many a good night down the pub with the blokes in order to keep her happy and wedding plan. Anyway, you don't seem like the other toffs who walk in here. I'll get you a mochaccino any time you need one.'

I sensed I was being made fun of for my coffee choice. Bert hunched his shoulders then exhaled while he walked out from behind the counter to turn the *Open* sign on the window to *Closed*. It was my cue to leave. He was a grumpy old sod and made awful coffee, but he appeared to be my only choice in caffeine fixes so I would be back.

Out on the street, while Bert closed the door behind me then pulled the curtains, I couldn't see Amelia. Hanging from a lamppost, however, was a sign *Homemade Fudge*. I knew my ex-wife and therefore walked straight into the shop – and had to hastily duck to avoid hitting my head on the door frame. The people who lived there hundreds of years ago were clearly vertically challenged.

Amelia was busy with the sample platters. 'This is Anne,' she told me. 'She makes the most delicious fudge I've ever tasted.'

'That is very generous. Good evening, Jamieson. I hear you're staying at The Pied? That's a lovely place. The locals like heading up there for a pint and a pub meal by the fire. I see you would have met Bert.' Anne spied my coffee cup. 'I hope you weren't put off this place by him – he's a grouchy old bastard. Would turn the tourists off in droves if he had his way. Doesn't understand that without tourists we have no livelihood. I could just shoot him sometimes, the way he talks to people. We've both been in business here for forty years. My mother started this fudge shop and Bert's father the coffee shop. They were close, you know, perhaps a little too close – created a scandal in their day. Had the village gossip mill alight with their midnight dalliances and secret rendezvous. Despite that though, they both knew how to run a good business and attract customers. Bert should be ashamed of himself.'

Wanting to change the topic, I asked for a piece of the double chocolate fudge. This holiday was not going to be good for my waistline.

Ding-dong, ding-dong, ding… it was the bells from the old stone church further down the lane.

'Isn't it wonderful to be in a place where the church bells still ring – not just for a special occasion?' Amelia was obviously enjoying herself.

'Five o'clock, it'll be,' said Anne. 'The bells ring the number of times corresponding to each hour. If it were winter it would be dark outside right now but look: it's still lovely and light. The sun won't set here till about nine o'clock – plenty of time for me to tend to my roses when I get home after work. Ta ta now.'

Stepping down onto the footpath outside the shop, I felt a chilly gust. It appeared that early summer in England could still be crisp. I pulled my jacket sides together, lowered my head, and we walked into the wind back to The Pied. Amelia chose to check into her room. I walked into the bar area and sank into the leather armchair by the – thankfully – roaring fire. A jar of marshmallows and long skewers had been placed at the side of the granite hearth. Tomorrow I would need to go for a run.

Chapter 3

'Hello, stranger!' It was Fraser, my detective friend from South Beach, looking a bit rougher than at home. The neat haircut had grown and the normal close shave had been replaced by what looked like two weeks' growth.

'What have you been up to?' I asked. 'I've never seen you look so relaxed.'

'This is what a good roll in the sack each day will do to a guy.'

'Eh?' Fraser had been without female company for years.

'Yes, it appears the women are a lot friskier over here than at home, and I am a very happy man. I've been in London for the past week and met a honey the first night I was there. I plan on catching up with her again after the wedding – sorry, renewal of vows, as Sam keeps reminding me. Same thing if you ask me. Speak of the devil.'

Sam had come into the pub area of the hotel and walked straight over to where Fraser and I were seated. 'Hey, no drinks yet? That's not like you two.'

'I needed to sit by the fire to defrost first.'

'What are you having? Drinks are on me – it's the least I can do since you flew halfway around the globe for our vow renewal.'

'Beer for me, but surprise me,' Fraser said. 'I'm keen to try some of the local craft stuff while we're here.'

'Bacardi and Coke,' I requested.

'I could have guessed that.' Sam had a bounce about him. 'By the way, we chose The Pied for everyone to stay at because it's owned by Clarence and Juliette, who both went to university with Tilda.' Sam gestured to a man behind the bar. 'That's Clarence there. British patriot to the core, he is. It's hard to imagine Tilda having another life here, in England, before she met me and we moved to South Beach. Anyway, she's wasting no time in filling up on Yorkshire puddings and Cornish pasties.'

Sam headed to the bar. He was too tall for the ceiling and needed to stoop under the exposed wooden beams. His curly, shaggy hair was out of place among the slick, well-dressed patrons. He returned – still looking like the cat who'd stolen a bucket of cream.

'How are you feeling, mate? Any pre-vow-renewal jitters?' I asked.

'None at all. Tilda and I have never been better together. You know how she was going through some kind of midlife crisis in South Beach and dressing all black, wearing dog chains and tattooing herself? Well, since returning to her home turf she has changed. She's dropped the black, covered the tattoos, and the dog chains are now in the bedroom! What hasn't changed is her quest to use sex to stay young. I can't believe my luck, really.'

I tried to delete the image of Sam, Tilda and chains from my mind.

'There is something in the air over here,' Fraser nodded. 'For once I'm not the guy sitting here with no stories to tell.'

'Have you hooked up with someone?' Sam looked startled.

'Yep. She's in London. Obviously it will all come to an end when I head home, but I'm going back there after leaving this village, to make hay while the sun shines.'

'How about you, Jamieson?' asked Sam. 'You've been here for more than an hour – you would have met someone by now.'

Is that really what he thinks of me? 'Actually, I did, but Amelia put an end to all of that.'

'Why did you introduce your ex-wife to your new woman?' Sam reached for a marshmallow.

'I didn't. Amelia found her shoes.'

'Where?'

'In my bathroom.'

'What was she doing in there?'

'She needed to go to the toilet.'

'And you let her in while you were entertaining?'

'What can I say? Amelia is persistent.'

'Whoa, awkward!'

'It was a little. Amelia steamrolled the poor woman.' At least, at home, Amelia and I had a strict rule of knocking on each other's door before entering so I didn't have to introduce her to my latest lust interest knowing she would subsequently hassle me about it – unless I stupidly chose to open the door like this time.

'Where is this woman now?' Fraser was interested.

'She left. She was here for her friend's twenty-first birthday party.'

'Twenty-first?' Sam coughed. 'Should I ask how old she is?'

'Twenty something? Early twenties? Let's just say it wasn't one of my finer choices.'

'I can see why Amelia would have gone off her rocker.' Fraser laughed.

'She got over the initial shock quite quickly,' I reflected. 'Might have been the jet-lag.'

'Pretty good to know you've still got it eh?' asked Sam. 'Pulling a twenty-something-year-old – not bad for a guy your age.'

'Yes, well, Amelia put an end to it all before it started. Gotta love having your ex-wife on holiday with you.'

'Come on, we all know you're still obsessed with Amelia and filling in time until she takes you back.'

'I hate to admit it, but you're right. Anyway, cheers to Sam and Tilda, may your future be bright and...'

'Full of bonks.'

'You're all class, Sam. Don't know how you fit in with Tilda's English society friends, but may your future be bright and fill of bonks.'

'Hear, hear.' Ching went the three glasses.

Chapter 4

I leaned back into the armchair and looked around the room. The Pied had originally been built in the fourteenth century and any renovation had clearly respected its original architecture. Not one wall was straight and the floor undulated. Built with the yellowish limestone called Cotswold stone, its walls were about twenty centimetres thick – enough to keep the cold out and the warmth in. Brown leather sofas and wooden tables and chairs as well as leaners occupied the space. The door kept opening and closing however – this was a busy establishment.

There were three distinct groups: the locals, I assumed, since they were wearing jumpers and fancy gumboots with a city-turned-country look about them; the London toffs, as Bert would call them, in chinos and open-top shirts, expensive watches and gelled hair; and what I could only assume were some vow-renewal guests of Sam and Tilda's that I had yet to meet.

Clarence came over. 'Good evening, I'm Clarence, my wife, Juliette and I own The Pied. Sam said you've flown in from South Beach. Welcome.'

Pleasantries aside, Clarence continued. 'I haven't always dreamed of owning a bed and breakfast, you know. It was an idea that just came to Juliette and me one morning. I was an investment banker at Goldman Sachs, living the high-life, doing deals involving pounds you wouldn't believe – crazy amounts of money sloshing around really. One morning when faced with rising at five am to start the day again, I looked at Juliette and said, "Honey, what am I doing? We're multi-millionaires. When am I going to call this quits and do something I really enjoy?" Juliette was in investor relations for British Gas and she'd had enough of dealing with demanding sharebrokers and fund managers and the like –' Clarence was starting to cut close to home '– so we both called in sick, something I'd never dreamt of doing before, and decided to look for a lifestyle change. It turned out to be perfect timing because The Pied was for sale. We bought it outright with cash so we have no mortgage on it. Bad idea really, we should get a mortgage and put some of the cash into shares – far better returns – but that is thinking for another day.'

'Jamieson's in your old business field,' Sam told him. 'He's a fund manager.'

'Jamieson? How many could there be? You're not *the* Jamieson Hart, are you?'

'It depends on the reputation that precedes me.'

'Goodness, you're well known and respected in Goldman Sachs' London office. Sinclair in our Singapore office always kept us updated on the work you were doing and the income stream it provided for Goldmans.'

'Ah yes, Sinclair and I have had some fun working on deals together. It is, as they say, a very small world.'

'It's a fish bowl at the top, and you, Jamieson, are a prominent global fish.'

It was nice to have my ego stroked but I wasn't sure I wanted it done by Clarence.

'You aren't just an ordinary fund manager, are you? You don't sit back and juggle portfolios – you've got skin in the game. You're like a private equity master as well, spying opportunities and restructuring companies to make outstanding returns. Who can beat a performance record of twenty percent per annum over the last ten years?'

'Whereas you've moved from investment banker to hotelier and publican.' I changed the topic. 'I hope you've found what you were looking for.'

'Without a doubt. If Juliette and I hadn't have acquired The Pied, I shiver to say that an immigrant would have most likely taken it. A Russian, maybe. The Russian oligarchs are buying up the country for investment purposes – using Britain as a hedge against their periodic economic crises. The Brits need to take back control before it's too late. It's like this whole Brexit thing. Who could be pro remaining in Europe? Britain needs to stand alone.'

Ah, that would explain the oversized Union Jack at the front of The Pied.

'It's the same with the wealthy Ukrainians – you know, buying up Britain. They shouldn't be allowed in the country.'

'Yet you seemed to have quite happily dealt with Sinclair in Goldman's Singapore office, as opposed to London brokers.' I noted.

'Yes, well, Sinclair was different. Who wouldn't like him? And I don't mind the financial borders being open so much – it's the property investment that needs to remain British. It is, after all, our land. Hold on a minute, I can see Juliette needs me. I'll be back later. As I said, welcome to The Pied and enjoy your evening.'

Clarence walked towards a fit-looking brunette wearing a dusky-pink dress. Presumably Juliette.

'Tilda's talked to me quite a lot about Clarence, but she's never mentioned how staunchly nationalistic he is,' said Sam.

'He's entitled to his opinions,' Fraser commented while yawning and stretching out his arms.

'I didn't expect them to come out so strongly.' Sam had a puzzled look on his face.

'I guess it's a hot topic here at the moment,' I said whilst feeling the need for another drink.

'Ah, these guys will be better to talk to,' said Sam, gesturing at an Indian couple entering the pub.

He lifted himself off his chair and shook hands with them, and introduced them to us as Samrina and Sanjay. 'Samrina is a management consultant with PwC and her current client is the BBC.' Sam was working hard on his introductions.

'That's right, the BBC is occupying a lot of my time,' Samrina agreed. 'We're trying to improve their business processes and install an enterprise-wide planning system. Being government run there's a lot of room for improvement. We see large scope for reducing costs in that organisation.'

'Does that mean redundancies?' Sam asked.

'There will be some – there always are on a job like this, unfortunately. I should keep my voice down in case there are some BBC employees here.'

Looking at the chinos and posh gumboot crowd, I doubted it.

Sam continued, 'And Sanjay is a Cambridge University lecturer on the philosophy of religion.'

'Sounds interesting,' I said. 'I've never met a lecturer in such an area. What exactly do you cover in the course?'

'We examine the themes and concepts involved in all the major religious traditions – Christianity, Islam, Buddhism, Hinduism. Quite passionate arguments can erupt in some of the lectures, I can tell you, but largely we try to keep it in the theoretical domain.'

'Tell me, how did you two and Clarence over there come to meet Tilda? Obviously not at lectures, since Tilda's a doctor.' I was intrigued.

'We were all at Cambridge,' Samrina answered. 'I shared a flat with Tilda in our third year, and Clarence took over my room when I moved out the following year to live with Sanjay. It's lovely to meet you. Sanjay and I have some work to do before we relax tomorrow, but we just wanted to put our heads in and say hello to Sam. We saw Tilda having her nails done in the spa –' I knew Amelia would be with Tilda '– and she told us you would be at the pub.'

Sam laughed. 'My wife knows me well.'

Samrina and Sanjay were just out of earshot when Fraser leaned towards me and Sam. 'Bloody heck, Sam, you didn't tell me I would be having to mix with the likes of ex-investment bankers, management consultants and Cambridge lecturers – I don't feel intellectually equipped for this holiday.'

'I know, what can I say? I feel like I need to be on my best behaviour. I can see why Tilda found England all a bit stuffy after a while.'

'A little bit! How am I going to pretend my way through these conversations? I don't even know exactly what it is Jamieson does, and he's a good mate. Hopefully you're going to introduce me to someone a bit more my level next.' Fraser downed his beer in one gulp.

It was nice to be away with these two. We drank, toasted marshmallows – slightly burnt on the outside, sticky in the middle – and then I hit the sack.

Chapter 5

I had forgotten to click my phone to silent for all calls except those of my kids. It rang at 5:30am.

It was Mirabelle, my rainbow-Lycra-clad, irrational Chilean housekeeper in South Beach who keeps me teetering on the edge of firing her. She has a heart of gold, I am sure; I am just privy to far too many insights about her annoying boyfriend Rodrigo.

'Mr Hart, it is I, Mirabelle. I ringing because it is so bad, Mr Hart. It bad news. I know not what to do so I call you.'

'What is it, Mirabelle?

'Your swimming pool, it go green. I no know why. I come here this morning, it green!'

'Don't worry about it – the recent rain has probably knocked the chemicals off balance. The pool guys are due tomorrow anyway. They'll fix it.' My bachelor pad is U-shaped around a masterpiece swimming pool that I never use since I am a beach swimmer.

'Oh dear.'

'What's the matter?'

'My Rodrigo.'

Shoot me.

'My Rodrigo is by the pool naked. You say it okay if we use your pool while you away. You so kind. Rodrigo ready but no can go. Oh, it's okay – we use spa pool instead. Thank you, Mr Hart, you are so kind boss.'

I felt my stomach's contents rise to my throat as I closed my phone. The spa would need emptying, scrubbing and fresh water added before I could get back in there after naked Rodrigo. Actually, maybe it was time to buy a new one?

With no beach for hundreds of kilometres here, my daily ocean swim or kayak needed to be replaced with a run. I put on my gear and headed out. It had obviously rained overnight since the ground was slightly soft under foot and the air smelled fresh and sweet. The sun had already risen but had yet to gain great distance from the horizon – it cast a yellow glow over the countryside.

I ran along the lanes, looking out beyond the metre-high, mostly intact stonewall to green meadows and rolling hills, bordered by blue sky. Bushes of white daisies had sewn themselves along parts of the wall and a chorus of cicadas was busy generating the sound of summer. The temperature was still a little chilly so I pulled my long-sleeved running top down over my hands for protection.

Apart from the insects, it was quiet. Gloriously quiet. Not a sound of a vehicle or people, just the noise of nature. I could understand why this place had hit the weekend radar of wealthy Londoners.

I should have meditated and stayed in each moment; instead my mind was drawn into determining a plan for Xtrapak. The CEO needed money and fast so he would be open to any suggestions I had to offer. I wanted the assets, and I wanted to shake up the board and realise Xtrapak's full potential.

Convertible debt. It hit me. I stopped running and pulled out my phone. Now I was the one disturbing the peaceful morning.

'Evening, Jamieson – or should I say morning where you are?'

I wasn't going to pretend this guy and I were friends; investment deals go a lot more smoothly without emotions involved. 'Wes, I have a proposition for you. Glasward-Sade Hart will issue you ten million in convertible debt. The period of issue is two years. At the end of this period, Glasward-Sade Hart either gets repaid in full in cash plus ten percent interest, or the outstanding debt is converted to equity and Glasward-Sade Hart will own shares in Xtrapak.'

'Blimey, ten million is too good to turn down — we can't raise five anywhere else.'

This guy should learn not to reveal his hand.

'But repaid in two years? That would be impossible.'

'An incentive, one might say, to turn the business around and generate some decent returns.'

'It would require a lot of work on my part.'

No kidding, Sherlock — that's why you get paid the big bucks each year.

'Yet, I just don't see another option.'

'Think on it for a couple of hours, then call me back.' It sounded like Wes had no better deal on the table — he wouldn't be able to scramble anything together within two hours.

As I closed my phone, I heard something rustling around to the side of a daisy bush, a small furry critter with a black-and-white striped face. I was leaning over the bush trying to get a closer look when I heard a voice behind me.

'It's a badger. Quite common around here, and largely considered pests, but I like them. It's cute, don't you think?'

Turning my head, I beheld a delightful pair of legs in red running shoes, then used every bit of strength in my thighs to reverse myself out of the bush without falling right in. 'I agree, and why any person would ever want to injure an animal is beyond me. My name is Jamieson.' I shook her hand.

'I'm Polly.'

I wanted to ask her if she needed to put the kettle on, then assumed she had heard that several times before and might be unimpressed by the cliché. 'Do you live around here?' I asked instead.

'No, I live in London. Taking a few days' holiday here – it's the one place I can come to and truly relax. The country air cures a multitude of ills. I'm staying at The Pied Piper – The Pied it's most often called.'

This was too good to be true. 'That's where I'm staying,' I told her.

'Are you here for the wedding? I'm not but it seems a lot of people are.'

'Yes – renewal of vows, I keep being reminded. My ex-wife is here too, which always makes things interesting.' Yes, I was fishing.

'I'm single.' Bingo. 'Just been through a break-up actually. It got nasty. We'd been together for five years. That's part of the reason why I had to leave London for a while – that and my work. I'm a barrister. Just won a case before a judge who had obvious biases, although they're supposed to be neutral. It was a hard slog but we got there in the end.'

'Congratulations.' I was squinting into the rising sun, trying to decide how old Polly was. Forty? With a standard deviation of five years? Sometimes it was hard to tell but the fact that she was a practising barrister put her safely out of the twenties age bracket – that hadn't worked out so well for me last time.

'Anyway,' she said, 'I'd better get on with my run. I might see you at The Pied later.'

Later was carried by the wind as the red shoes jogged away from me.

I brushed off a few of the daisy leaves that had stuck to my shorts and decided it was time to leave the badger and set off running again. The phone rang. This time it was the kids. Always a pleasure. Their grandparents had been spoiling them with sailing trips, hiking adventures and loads of hot chocolates. They were happy and therefore so was I. The Cotswolds were going to suit me just fine.

Chapter 6

My run took longer than I'd planned. The scenery was spectacular and I wanted to burn off some of last night's marshmallows before trying to charm Polly later.

Sam and Tilda (a respiratory specialist whom I affectionately call 'the good doctor') were standing with an athletic looking bloke on The Pied's gravel path when I returned.

'Jamieson, let me introduce you to Jordan Sticks,' said Tilda. 'You've probably heard of him – he's Ramlock United's star soccer player.'

'I have watched many of your games – the last one against Lazio was pretty tough. Well done on the penalty shootout.' I was a little star struck.

'Cheers, man.'

Polly approached us. 'Excuse me – Jordan Sticks? My nephew is obsessed with you. May I bother you for a photo? Jamieson, would you mind?'

How could I say no? I duly took the photo, then, as Polly walked away, Jordan irritated me by saying, 'Aw, she's a bit of all right, isn't she? Tilda, is she another friend of yours?'

'No.'

'Fair play then.'

It wasn't fair at all. This was in no way going to be a level playing field. I would have to do a lot of work on my marketing for Polly.

Tilda continued, 'Jordan and I lived next door to each other in Richmond Park when we were young. We've kept in touch ever since.'

I was starting to think my shaggy-haired friend had done quite well in gaining the affection of Tilda – she had been well-exposed to a variety of eligible men, it seemed. Sam must have been her ticket to a world unknown. No wonder they ended up arguing a lot in South Beach – perhaps the grass hadn't been greener after all for her?

'Have you got a break in training?' I asked Jordan.

'Yes, a couple of weeks. Means I get to come up here and congratulate Tilda and Sam. There are worse places I could spend time during my break, that's for sure.'

I excused myself to return to my room for a shower, bumping into my ex-wife, Amelia, on the way.

'Oh, my goodness, did you see Jordan Sticks is here!'

'Yes.'

'He is hot!'

'Is he?'

'Come on, Jordan Sticks – are you serious? I'm going to enjoy Sam and Tilda's vow renewal all the more now.'

'Excellent. I'm heading for the shower.'

'I talked to the kids this morning. They seem happy – Mum and Dad have them sorted.'

'Yes, I spoke to them too. All good.' I shut my suite door behind me.

Forming a puddle on the floor from the shower, I answered my phone. It was Wes from Xtrapak.

'What can I say, Jamieson? You have me stuck between a rock and a hard place. I don't want to give up shares in Xtrapak but I have no option other than to accept your offer of convertible debt.'

Some gratitude. 'Nice to be in business with you, Wes,' I lied. 'My team in the Singapore office will be in contact to sort the details. And remember – if Xtrapak performs well over the next couple of years I will happily walk away with cash and no shares.'

'We both know it won't perform any better than now.'

And that, my friend, is why I am very happy with this deal, I thought as I closed my phone. In two years' time, I expected my number of shares would give me a controlling stake in Xtrapak. The board was going to experience a big shuffle and Wes would be the first casualty. I already had a plan for whom I would make chairman of the board – a cunning, older fox I had worked with on previous projects. Xtrapak's potential would be realised and I would be a happy man. In the meantime, I would maintain a civil approach towards Wes and his board of baboons.

I called Penelope, my work sidekick.

'Helloooo, Jamieson.'

That drawl – what was with that? 'Penelope, I need you to engage with Wes from Xtrapak.' I ran through the deal we had just made.

'No worries. How is life in the Cotswolds treating you?'

'I think I will be quite happy here,' I replied, hoping I would get somewhere with Polly.

A note was slid under my door.

Sam and Tilda would love the pleasure of your company at a picnic they will be holding today at North-Mile Woods, one kilometre from The Pied. It can be accessed by walking north across the grass from the back of the hotel. Staff members have been briefed and can point you in the right direction if need be. Lunch will be at 1pm. Tilda and Samuel.

Samuel? Tilda really was reverting to her roots, I wondered if Sam might struggle a bit with that.

It wasn't a grab-a-blanket-and-sit-on-the-grass picnic. Tables and chairs with white cloths were set out under a grouping of willow trees. A string quartet played and waiters circulated with champagne and hors d'oeuvres.

Fraser approached me. 'Jeepers, am I pleased you made it, Jamieson. Can you believe the effort that went into this shindig?'

'Yes, not quite what I was expecting, but that rare beef and cucumber canape looks good,' I said as I reached for the tray. 'Hi, Sam.' He had walked over to join Fraser and me.

'Aargh, thank you for calling me Sam – everyone's started calling me Samuel! I haven't been called that since I was being told off by my mother.

Tilda doesn't even call me that when we're in South Beach – she's gone all weird and posh on me. I can't say I'm enjoying it.'

'Maybe she'll go back to the way she was when she gets home. Does she feel pressured to be something she's not when she's here?' I suggested.

'Well, she's pretending somewhere – here or at home. I just hope it's here.'

'I'm sure you guys will get through this. Not that I am in any way equipped to offer marriage advice.'

'I might be needing divorce advice if Tilda continues this way – I don't know what she's playing at.'

'Look, mate, I get you. I feel as comfortable here as a person with two left feet doing the first dance at a ball,' Fraser said. 'But Tilda's a good woman, you know that. Give her the benefit of the doubt and talk to her. I'm sure it'll all work out.'

'I hope you're right, Fraser,' said Sam as he headed to the drinks table.

'Totally lied there,' Fraser admitted. 'I would have no interest in any woman who laid this kind of hoity-toity bullshit on me. I like my women grounded to earth. I don't know what Tilda's thinking.'

At this point Sam returned with yet another guy dressed in a long-sleeved shirt, chinos and boat shoes, sweating in the sun but clearly unwilling to remove his pinstriped jacket.

'Jamieson, Fraser, let me introduce Donald Crabshaw.'

I could imagine Fraser beside me choking on his olive.

'Good afternoon, gentlemen, it is a pleasure to meet you. My family and Tilda's go back a long way, though I really got to know her at Cambridge. Tilda was studying medicine and I was studying finance. I am a hedge fund manager – a tough job but someone has to do it. It requires a special kind of skill, you know, an ability to search out good opportunities and be ready to pounce when the time is right. Not a job for the average plebe. So, what is it you two do?'

Fraser really did start choking and Sam was far too quick to offer to go with him to get some water, leaving me with Donald Crabshaw.

I wasn't in the mood to play a game of one-upmanship with this guy. 'You must know Clarence then?' I asked. 'The owner of The Pied who was once an investment banker?'

'I certainly do, although I don't understand why one would ever leave the world of banking to run a hotel and pub – don't understand that malarkey at all. Who would want to leave London to live here, in the middle of nowhere? Clarence says he likes it. I daresay his wife Juliette "puts out" a lot in order to keep him here.'

Donald was quite possibly the worst human I had ever met.

He made the mistake of asking, 'You never told, what is it you do?'

'I'm a fund manager, private wealth, based with Glasward-Sade Hart out of Singapore.'

'Jamieson Hart?'

'Yes.'

'Why, I know who you are. You'll be interested in this – I have just returned from a trip to New York. I went to the Berkshire Hathaway meeting and saw Warren Buffet in action. Formidable man. What was most interesting was…'

I have never been happier to see my ex-wife hobbling towards me.

'Ah, Jamieson, why did I choose to wear these heels, for goodness sake? They're new and they're giving me blisters – I'm already wearing four plasters, and the heels are so thin they keep sinking into the dirt every time I step. It's like I have suction pads attached to my feet. Sorry,' she added to Donald, 'I should introduce myself. I'm Amelia.'

'Good afternoon. I am Donald Crabshaw.' Exuding disapproval of Amelia's interruption, Donald, to my relief, turned and walked away.

'What's up with him?' Amelia asked.

'He doesn't appreciate fine women.' I smiled.

'What's up with you?'

'Not a thing.' In that moment with Amelia partially sunk into the ground, a box of plasters in one hand and a perplexed look on her face, I fell in love with my ex-wife for the millionth time.

Chapter 7

'Oh, thank goodness.' Amelia gestured at Sanjay and Samrina approaching. 'These two are the best of a bad bunch.'

Never backward in coming forward, she greeted them with, 'Hello, I'm just wondering what makes you two so normal, considering the other company we have here?'

'Ha, yes, we saw you talking to Donald Crabshaw and thought you might need some light relief,' Sanjay replied.

'Why does he get called Donald Crabshaw? Would Donald not suffice?' Amelia asked.

Samrina shrugged. 'He's been Donald Crabshaw as long as I've known him. Who knows why? It kind of suits him though. He was born to a very wealthy family and doesn't know a life any different. I think he respects me because I did better than him at university – crushed his pride being beaten by a woman. Also, a management consultant appears to be an acceptable job in Donald Crabshaw's hierarchy.'

'I get a look-in because *Cambridge lecturer* is in my job title. If I lectured at any other university I doubt he'd give me the time of day.' Sanjay added.

'God, what a miserable life he must lead.' Amelia shoved her plasters back in her handbag. 'Oh, goodness, I'm sorry, Sanjay – I forgot who I was talking to.'

'Ah, no need to apologise. Lecturing in religious studies does not mean I am religious.'

'Huh? I would have thought they went hand in hand.'

'Not at all. I have always been interested in human nature and group thought, and I'm fascinated by the formation of organised belief systems – how each came into being and how they continue to be relevant today. Personally, I am not religious at all. Spiritual definitely, but I do not subscribe to rituals or set systems of beliefs.'

'It's fascinating how different the faces of major religions are today compared to hundreds of years ago.' Amelia used my arm for balance as she tried to unstick her shoe.

Sanjay nodded agreement. 'Just like a business, they have all had to evolve to stay relevant. Take Christianity and Islam, for instance. Both initially had strong views on the role of women in society that would be unacceptable in a modern, western environment. Of course, some religions have evolved more than others. It's not a topic I generally talk about at dinner parties since one of two outcomes tend to occur. Any devout religious person in a group will approach me and start quoting scripture under the misapprehension that we are on the same "team"; or I notice an ever-widening empty circle around me as I am identified as a "religious freak", incapable of having a good time.'

'Did I hear someone talking about a good time?' A man in his seventies, at a guess, with wiry hair and clad in a beige herringbone jacket stumbled from behind the low-lying willow branches. He almost looked like he'd been dribbling. 'My name ish Norrie. I am Tilda'sh uncle.'

Tilda's uncle Norrie had definitely been enjoying the booze.

'And who would this picture of beauty before me be?' He was looking at Amelia. 'Iiii've beena watching you frooooom a distance. Easy on the eye, you are.'

I thought Amelia was going to hit him.

'Serioussssly, look at the tosshie.' The bum squeeze sent her over the edge. Only the fact that Norrie was Tilda's uncle saved him from what Amelia was capable of unleashing at this point. She unplugged her heels again from the mud and walked away, Sanjay and Samrina going with her.

'A bit ruuude, isn't she?' Saliva formed a line on the side of Uncle Norrie's chin. 'They make them feisty where you're from, do they?' He grabbed hold of a willow branch to aid his balance. 'Anyway, I hear you are Jamiessssson Hart?'

'Yes, that's right.'

'I know, you sssseee. I know who you arrrre, because I follow the shhhhharemarket, you sseeeee. Have my own porrrrtfolio.'

Was that his spit that had landed on my face? I hoped it was water dripping from a leaf.

'You are a leeegendarryy investor. Oh, look, there is Jordan Sticks!' Uncle Norrie sounded more sober. 'He plaaaays for Ramlock Uniiiited, the soccer team. Big businessssss here in the UK – I have invesssted quite a few pounds in them.'

Another spit. This time, I wasn't too polite to wipe my face.

'They should have a good seassssson. I am counting on iiiit. My wife died, you knoooow, ssssssoo now I ssspend a lot of time invesssting and tryyyying to get a young filly like that one over theeeeere.' He pointed towards Amelia who returned his goggle with a look like she was sucking lemons.

'I don't rate your chances there,' I advised him.

'Can't blaaame a maaan for ttttrying, caaan you?'

I guess not but I was getting near my expiry time for this party. I'd thought things couldn't get worse but then Clarence and Juliette approached, Clarence wearing a Union Jack pin on his suit jacket.

'You see, this is why we need to keep British land in British hands – picnics like this would be relics of the past if we sold out to Russians and Ukrainians and all the rest.'

Clarence's voice became white noise as Polly walked by. She wasn't part of the vow-renewal party but had obviously decided to ramble this way. Her dark hair was pulled back in a ponytail and she was wearing a pale-blue cotton shirt over jeans that were tucked into knee-high boots. What the heck, Jordan Sticks had walked over to join her!

I couldn't approach her as well, that would be encroaching on another man's turf – and anyway I wasn't going to mess with the physicality of Jordan Sticks. Instead, I had the pleasure of watching the Jordan-Polly show while being bored to tears by Clarence and every so often having to give Uncle Norrie a nudge to keep him vertical.

Fraser and Sam walked past, Fraser asking, 'Jamieson, want to skip the rest of this and walk back to the pub?'

Without a doubt. Amelia was talking to Tilda, Polly was looking too interested in what Jordan Sticks had to say, and everyone else at the picnic was irrelevant. I was delighted to walk out from under the shade of the willows and into the sunshine.

On the way to the pub at The Pied, I veered off from Fraser and Sam and called into Bert's coffee house. Cheap supermarket fudge – still in its distribution box – languished on the counter.

'A coffee, thanks, Bert.' I knew better than to ask for a mochaccino.

'Coming right up. Can I interest you in some homemade fudge?'

'Come on, Bert, we both know that's as homemade as my socks.'

'Is it that obvious?'

'Yes.'

'Anne keeps taking all my customers. They walk here to get a coffee, see fudge next door and go to her instead. I have to compete.'

I held back from suggesting he focused on trying to make decent coffees.

Stepping out of the shop, I flashed back to a phone call I'd had with Sandra, my business partner, a few weeks earlier.

Jamieson, I have something that will make you happy and something else I need to tell you.'

'Sounds ominous. What will make me happy?'

'I just landed a new client, ten mill worth. The couple from rural New South Wales I visited a few weeks ago has signed.'

'Excellent. Now what should I brace myself for?'

'I have to tell you now since I'm the only one in the office – I don't want anyone else to know. I need some cash. A few property investments of mine have not gone as well as I'd hoped and all my spare cash is tied up in unbreakable assets. I'm starting to feel the pinch. It's embarrassing – to say the least – to have to tell you this.'

'How can I help?'

'I would like us to list Glasward-Sade Hart on the sharemarket.' Silence while Sandra waited for my response.

'Okay, so that has caught me by surprise. I am going to need time to think about it.'

'Of course, but the less time you need the better. I'm sorry to hit you with this but I truly am in a bind.'

'Do you really want to be answerable to shareholders?'

'I don't think I have a choice.'

I must say, the idea of issuing shares to the firm and banking the cash had some appeal. 'What's your proposal?'

'You and I keep a seventy percent stake and we list the remaining thirty. I reckon if we issue two and a half million shares we should get about seven-dollars-fifty a share.'

'You think the firm is worth —' I *quickly calculated '—roughly sixty million?'*

'On the day of release at least, and upwards from there.'

'Let me think on it.'

I had closed my phone, a cautiously happy man.

The listing process involving brokers, lawyers and the stock exchange was now underway, led by Sinclair, my friend in the Singapore office of Goldman Sachs. The extra cash generated from listing the firm would go a long way in a new investment idea I was pondering.

Chapter 8

The sun was out and so were tables and chairs in front of The Pied. Fraser and Sam had already started on beers. I joined them and ordered myself a Heineken; it's rare that I break from Bacardi. I held up my bottle to cheers.

'Cheers to the biggest disaster trip ever.' Sam was rubbing his head with his hands.

'Whoa, mate, what's going on?' I asked.

'What's going on? I left the kids at home with a nanny to come here, to Tilda's home country to reconnect with her and renew our vows, but I don't think I want to do that anymore. I hate to say it but I think Tilda's a snob, judging by her old friends. I have absolutely nothing in common with them, and Tilda has turned into someone different here.'

'They're a bunch of snobby twats, if you ask me,' Fraser concurred.

'I don't know if that's very helpful.' I slumped further into my seat.

'Fraser's right,' said Sam. 'Who in their right mind would want to mix with those people?'

'Tilda. Which means they can't be all that bad.' I was trying to sound upbeat – hard to do as I flashed back to Donald Crabshaw's disapproving look at Amelia.

'Tilda's changed. Today all she's cared about is what I wear and what I say, and she's started wearing stuck-up Englishy clothes. She never bothered about any of that in South Beach. And have you heard how she's talking now? I'm beginning to wonder if there really is a plum in her mouth. I just want my Tilda back – the one in South Beach. She was way more fun than this one.' Sam put his head on the table.

Fraser looked sympathetic. 'Wish I could help you here, mate, but I can't – I totally agree with you. Run while you can.'

'Okay, let's just calm down,' I intervened. 'Tilda married you for a reason in the first place, and she moved to South Beach to be with you.'

'But I'm nothing like those people she's hanging out with.'

'Samrina and Sanjay aren't bad. Anyway, maybe after a few more days with these people she will again want to leave it all behind and run away with you to South Beach,' I said optimistically.

'I hope you're right. Think I'll crash on your pull-out sofa tonight, Jamieson.'

'Are you sure that's wise? Won't you be fuelling a fire with Tilda when you don't turn up at the room?'

'No. I had a feeling I'd need an option out earlier, so I said to her that you, me and Fraser were going to have a boys' night in your suite and crash there – a bit of a stag, really.'

'Worst stag I've ever been to,' said Fraser.

'Cheers to that.' Sam raised his glass.

Thump thump. Someone was trying to bang the door down.

I opened my eyes, was partially blinded by the morning light but could see beer bottles scattered though the suite, with Sam on the couch and Fraser passed out on the floor. I guessed it was my darling ex-wife so I rubbed my eyes and walked in my boxer shorts to open the door.

'Fuck me, is that how you always open the door?' Tilda wasn't sounding quite so posh now. 'Where's Sam? Something awful has happened. It stinks in here – how much did you guys drink?'

'Tilda, honey, what's going on?' Sam was clearly happy to see this side of Tilda return.

'Uncle Norrie is dead!'

'Oh, for fuck's sake.' Fraser rolled over on the floor, holding his head. 'Why does work have to follow me wherever I go?' Fraser is a detective at home in South Beach. He buried his head under the pillow briefly, then squinted at her – clearly the light was too bright with a hangover. 'Sorry, Tilda, terrible reaction.'

Tilda had looked shocked at first, then decided to ignore him. 'Donald Crabshaw thinks Uncle Norrie had a heart attack.'

'All heil the Donald.'

Fraser was not being helpful but I had to laugh.

Fraser added, 'If Donald says it was a heart attack, a heart attack it must have been. Poor Uncle Nozza – I'm going back to sleep.'

'Tilda, that is awful. I am so sorry.' Sam scrambled off the couch, fought off what appeared to be light-headedness, then pulled Tilda towards him.

'Thank goodness Barbara and Veda arrived last night. They are Uncle Norrie's sisters – they hate being called aunties. Anyway, they're with his body now. How could this have happened? Poor Uncle Norrie.'

'Doesn't take a scientist to figure out what happened. Overweight, in his seventies, clearly ate everything dripping in cholesterol, drunk.'

'Fraser, stop! Come on, Tilda, let's go and see what we can do to help.' Sam was trying his hardest.

Tilda recoiled. 'You're dressed but aren't you going to brush your teeth first?'

Sam looked at me hopefully.

'Nope, you're going to have to go back to your room for your toothbrush, mate. We're close but not that close.' I was adamant.

'Norrie's not going to care,' Sam said to Tilda as he led her from the room and closed the door.

'Right, get that arse of yours off the floor. We need to go and pay our respects,' I said to Fraser as I battled my own desire to get back to bed.

'Really?'

'Yes, and try to be civil this time.'

'Aargh, worst holiday ever. I want to go back to London and shag Lucy.'

'Lucy? I never did ask you her name.'

'She's been sending me sex pics. It's torture staying here with this lot when Lucy's hot for me in London.'

I reflected on my lack of female company. Having Fraser sprawled out on my floor surrounded by beer bottles was not normally my style – and nothing was going to change in the sex department until he'd been evicted.

Uncle Norrie's body was laid on a bed in one of the spare rooms. Clarence was pacing, looking rather stressed. 'I hope they move the body soon – this is not at all good for business. Some people wouldn't contemplate staying if they knew a person had died here.'

'Norrie is not going anywhere,' stated a woman wearing gumboots, baggy green pants and a black singlet top. She had ruffled hair and no makeup. She said to Fraser and me, 'Good morning. I am Veda and this is Barbara.'

Ah, Norrie's sisters.

'What do you mean he's not going anywhere?' Barbara demanded. She wore oversized glasses and a jacket-and-pants suit with a clutch handbag. She had a hair-sprayed do and appeared to have emptied the foundation jar on her face.

'We are going to leave his body here until the vow renewals. Then everyone can come and talk to him, get close to him and say a proper goodbye,' said Veda.

'Nonsense. I am calling a funeral director now to come and remove Norrice's body. May he rest in peace.' Barbara pulled her phone from her handbag.

'Barbara, he will not rest in peace in a funeral home.'

'Veda, would you stop it with all this new-age stuff of yours and just leave it to me. No one wants a dead body nearby.' Barbara was flustered.

'Why not? Up until about a hundred years ago everyone died at home and the body stayed there until the funeral. It's only since the invention of medical technology and hospitals that people have started dying away from home and been carried off to morgues. Why should death be so inhuman?'

'Oh, my gosh. What would the Queen think?'

Eh? Barbara may have been missing a few pencils in the box.

'Who cares what the Queen would think?'

I agreed with Veda.

'She is the ruler of our empire! How dare you disrespect her?'

Fraser mimed shooting himself in the head with a gun, then fell backward onto an armchair.

'Hi, Jamieson, Fraser.' Tilda came to join us. 'I can see you've met my aunties, Veda and Barbara.'

'Yes, a pleasure in unfortunate circumstances,' I replied, not knowing what else to say.

I needed to take a break from this circus so stepped outside to call Kenneth Chow. He was a Singaporean billionaire I had partnered with on previous investment deals. I had a proposition for him.

Chapter 9

'Jamieson, I always get excited when I see your number – you have such intriguing propositions for me.'

I liked Kenneth Chow. 'Hopefully you find this one interesting. I may have an opportunity to start a Berkshire Hathaway type investment company and I am wondering, hypothetically, if you would be interested?'

'Continue.'

'Sandra, my business partner at Glasward-Sade Hart, and I are listing thirty percent of the firm. The cash from the float will put me in the position of being a serious personal investor. Just as Buffet did, I would like to buy a business, turn it around, then use the profits generated to invest in other businesses. It would be for my purposes only, not as part of Glasward-Sade Hart.'

'Wouldn't that put you in an ethical investing dilemma with Glasward-Sade Hart?'

'Not if I step down from the chief investment officer role, and take a seat on the board. I'm just thinking through the options.'

'I see. What company are you thinking of acquiring first as the investment vehicle?'

'Xtrapak.'

'Didn't you just issue convertible debt to them?' Kenneth was certainly on top of the market.

'Yes, but let's face it, Xtrapak's headed for a downward dive – the management is incapable. The board knows this but they too are incapable. Wes, the CEO, is a stickler but I think with enough financial incentive we'd be able to persuade him to leave.'

'We?'

'Yes.'

'How much are we talking here?'

'Partnership, twenty mill each.'

'Done.'

'Excuse me?'

'Done. I'm not going to blink, Jamieson, I have met a gazillion fund managers in my time and you're the only one I have any respect for. If you've found a good opportunity, I want to tag along for the ride.'

'I appreciate your backing here, Kenneth. The Glasward-Sade Hart float is tomorrow, Singapore time, and I won't know for sure how much cash I'll have available until it's listed.'

'Just keep talking to me as you go, Jamieson, but I am in when required.'

I closed my phone in admiration for someone who could make spontaneous decisions with such large amounts of money – though I guessed it was a drop in the ocean for a billionaire.

My thoughts were pleasantly interrupted by the sight of Polly walking towards me.

'Jamieson, do you know what happened here?'

'Yes, the uncle of the effective bride-to-be had a heart attack last night and died.'

'Really?'

'Unfortunately, yes.'

'And it was definitely a heart attack?'

'Well, that's what I've been told.'

'Oh, good.' She caught herself. 'Ooh, sorry, what an awful thing to say! It's just that I'm a single woman, only here for a few days, and I didn't want to stick around if it were something more sinister.'

It was good news that she still called herself single – maybe luck hadn't gone Jordan Sticks' way when he tried to charm her under the willows? 'I'm heading down to the shops for a coffee. Would you like to join me?' I had a window and was going to take it.

'Sure, why not? It's wonderful having nothing to do with my days.'

'You just finished a tricky case, didn't you say?'

'Yes – a sabotage case actually. Involved a major pie factory. One of the employees had been paid by a competitor to put cockroaches in the pies during the production process. It was all over the media here a year or so ago. Customers are very quick to complain about insects in pies.'

'Rightly so.'

'The company's sales collapsed overnight. It turned out to be a surprisingly hard task to prove sabotage but we got there in the end and I believe it was a fair result.'

'You must be feeling very satisfied then.'

'In the work department, yes. Personal area, not so much – haven't had much under-the-sheet action lately.' Polly winked.

You are kidding me. Opportunity had never come more easily.

'I was wondering what it was like to kiss a foreigner.' Polly had smutty eyes.

'Really? I'm sure you've kissed many foreigners before.'

'Not one as sexy as you.'

Who needed twenty-something-year-olds? Barristers in their forties suited me just fine. The sun broke through the clouds and warmed my back as I nudged Polly to the edge of a daisy bush and kissed her so she would never forget what it was like to kiss a non-Brit.

Frustratingly aware of a lack of privacy, given I was in a mood to do it au naturel, we then continued along the edge of the stream, heading towards the main line of shops.

The contradictions were stark. A mother duck and her babies took a leap of faith as they jumped off the bridge into the water; a bright yellow Lamborghini was parked on the corner where the gravel lane we were walking down joined onto the main one; Bert was putting out his *Coffee Here* sign; a tractor drove past with dogs on the tray; a woman with a recent boob-job stood waiting for a chino-clad, Ray-Ban-wearing guy to stop talking all-importantly down his phone; and the church bells rang to signal eight o'clock.

'I wonder what the locals think of us London tourists?' Polly asked.

'Probably depends on who you ask,' I truthfully replied.

'Feel like some fudge?'

'At 8am?'

'Who's counting time?'

The bell above the door jingled as we walked into Anne's fudge shop. Sugar and cocoa shouldn't smell so good this early in the morning.

'Morning. Beautiful day, isn't it? So lovely to have early morning tourists here – you must have left London at the break of dawn?' Anne was asking Polly.

'No, actually – I'm staying at The Pied. Not in the same group as Jamieson, though. We have just met.'

'Oh, I see.' Anne had a knowing look on her face.

Suddenly I felt like a kid who'd just pashed my girlfriend on the street, then taken her to the candy shop.

'Beware of the thieving Bert next door if you go to get coffee. He is now selling fudge. I cannot believe it. My loyal customers have told me it's rubbish stuff so that's good news, I guess. Smug bastard to think he could beat me at my own fudge game – I've been doing this for thirty years! Sorry, I shouldn't bore you with my problems. The sun is out – enjoy your day.'

I really did need Bert's brown-liquid, barely passable caffeine hit.

'More tourists today, did you notice?' asked Bert. 'Clogging up the lanes with their cars and walking around on their phones, making everyone else feel borderline stink. I don't know who they think they are.'

'Cheers for the coffee, Bert.'

Polly and I left before getting too caught up in his whinge-fest.

'So,' said Polly. 'It's a glorious day – look, they're even hanging bunting from the trees, the stream is trickling like something out of an Enid Blyton story, and we are both here with not much to do. Want to go back to your room and shag?'

Polly's personality was perplexing – but I had no intention of trying to figure her out. The walk along the lane back to my room took half the time it had on the way out.

'So now I know what it is like to be with a foreigner,' Polly said later.

She's a little weird. This foreigner thing could potentially get annoying, I thought as I left her stretched out on the bed while I headed to the shower.

She called after me, 'You don't want to stay here all day with me? I'm pretty good at acting if you're into roleplays?'

'Not really my thing, sorry,' I responded from the bathroom entrance.

'Bit of a prude, are you?'

I'd been called many things in my life, but never a prude.

'Come on, I have some cream in my bag – I always keep it there in case it's needed for occasions like this. The day's just started. You and me, pilot and air hostess, doctor and nurse, pimp and prostitute – what do you think?'

I just wasn't into it.

'Jamieson, Jamieson!' Amelia called just as I heard the lock click.

The woman had appallingly bad timing. I had forgotten I'd given her a key when she moved her bags from my room on arrival night. Soon enough, I was standing naked in the bathroom doorframe and Polly was on her knees with a can of cream when Amelia entered the room – the door behind her open, exposing some sheep grazing in the meadow.

'Oh, my goodness, you have got to be kidding me. What is wrong with you?' Amelia expostulated, and – as I grabbed a towel to cover myself – added, 'Don't bother, I've seen it all before, and apparently so has this lovely lady. Feeling a bit hungry, were you? Needed some cream? Jamieson can get a bit lactose intolerant sometimes so you may want to go easy on the quantities – he may burp it back all over you.'

'Amelia, why were you pounding on the door?'

'To talk to you about Tilda and Sam, and Norrie – the guy who died of a heart attack last night, remember? And the kids.'

'You have kids together?' Polly spoke.

'Yes, this is my ex-wife, Amelia. Perhaps this is not the best location for an introduction.'

'You reckon?' Amelia snapped. 'I'm heading back to my room. Come over when you're done with whatever you were doing here ... aargh, I don't want to think about it.' She closed the door behind her.

Was she angry because she still liked me? Was this jealousy?

'Oh, well, is it pimp and prostitute?' Polly started spraying cream.

'No. As much as I've enjoyed this, it's time for you to go.'

'Fine, I'll take my toolkit elsewhere.'

I showered then went to Amelia's room.

'You're clearly enjoying your time in the Cotswolds, aren't you?' Amelia walked over to the bench to pour a cup of tea.

'She seemed quite normal and keen. What's a warm-blooded guy to do? Then it all went a bit pear-shaped.'

'You prefer your cream on raisin toast?' Amelia had relaxed and was laughing.

'Definitely.'

'Tea?'

'Yes, please.' Amelia would always be my soft place to fall after all stupid decisions in my life.

My phone rang. 'It's Mirabelle. Do you want to talk to her?'

'Why would I want to talk to your housekeeper?'

I gave up and answered it.

'Morning, Mr Hart, it is I, Mirabelle. I ringing because your pool not green now. It is all good. Rodrigo and I, we go swimming. It so nice, we thank you very much. We like the spa pool most – it is very romantique.'

The spa was being replaced.

'I saw the mother of Mrs Hart –' that would be my ex-mother-in-law '– and she say Mrs Hart call her and say a man had heart attack where you staying. That no right, Mr Hart. I have very bad feeling. Might be a murder. You need be careful!'

'I can assure you he did have a heart attack and I am in no danger whatsoever – aside from being attacked by a badger.'

'You are silly silly man, Mr Hart. You must be careful.'

'Thank you, Mirabelle. I must go now.' I closed my phone and looked at Amelia. 'Did you have to tell your folks that Norrie died last night? Mirabelle will be on my back about this for the rest of the stay.'

'Of course. They were telling me about the kids and asking how things were – I couldn't omit a death. I can't help it if your housekeeper's going to talk to my folks and spin off irrationally like she does. Why do you still employ her?'

'It's easy.'

'You mean you're too lazy to change?'

'No, I mean I have enough volatility and stress in my work-life. I need my home-life to be stable.'

'I need more than a cup of tea.' Amelia yawned. 'I'm so tired – I was up most of the night talking to Tilda. She's having a hard time trying to figure out who she is and whether Sam or her old friends are more her type.'

'What was her conclusion?'

'Sam, I'm pretty sure, after a long road of alcohol-fuelled rumination. Think I'll have a sleep.'

I left Amelia and headed out to get some fresh air.

Chapter 10

An old oak was too appealing and I soon found myself lying in the shade of its branches, watching a group of people who'd decided to set up a cricket game on the grass area out the back of The Pied. A few sheep were diligently going about their job of keeping the grass short. It was a very English scene, and the sound of leather on willow combined with the chirping of cicadas carried me into an afternoon slumber.

I opened my eyes to realise I was the middle of a circle of jodhpur-clad busybodies talking about me.

'Oh, thank the Lord, he's not dead.' That was Barbara.

'However strange is that, to sleep in an open public space?' Clarence had joined in. 'Maybe this is how he comes up with great investment ideas?'

'Wouldn't want to be seen here though, would you? Very common behaviour, if you ask me, no matter even if you are one of the world's greatest investors.' It was Donald Crabshaw's turn.

'Some cultures thrive on afternoon naps. Meditation in nature is a core theme of Buddhism.'

Thank you, Sanjay.

'I wish I could go to sleep as easily as that – my mind won't stop ticking over enough to let it happen.' Samrina's contribution.

'I can't imagine this would ever happen to the royal family,' Barbara added.

'What wouldn't happen?' Veda asked.

'Someone disgracing themselves like this.'

'How on earth is sleeping in nature disgracing yourself? We are all part of the same energy, we are all one, and it is in nature that we truly ground and find ourselves.'

I quite liked Veda.

'Oh, gosh, imagine if the queen could hear you?'

Barbara really was deluded and these people had become tiresome. I got up, brushed bits of leaves and bark from my shorts and acted like nothing out of the ordinary had happened. In the distance, I saw Polly looking very cosy with Jordan Sticks. Maybe I was still dreaming. No, Donald Crabshaw's pinstriped jodhpurs were very real. I wondered if Jordan liked cream? I could happily function minus Polly.

Juliette arrived with a bag of helmets and I started to get a bad feeling. 'What are you all doing here?' I asked.

'Horse-riding,' Samrina replied. 'Tilda and Sam thought it would be a nice idea for us all to go for a ride – take our minds off what happened to her poor Uncle Norrie.'

Sam had never ridden a horse in his life so I doubted this would have been his idea.

'Poor old Norrice,' Barbara started. 'He was such a good man until his wife, Camille, died and then he just fell apart. Sad, really. He was an astute man in his heyday, good at investments and that sort of thing, you know – accumulated a lot of wealth. But one mustn't talk about money. That would be far too common.'

'Jamieson would have been interested in talking to Norrie,' Donald Crabshaw interjected. 'He really was an investment gun in his day – had a sharp eye for a good deal, one might say. Funny old fellow though, never did stop trying his luck with the ladies. Was always looking for ways to get a bit of pleasure action.'

This group was sucking the life out of me. Seeing Fraser and Amelia walking our way, I excused myself.

'I thought you were having a sleep?' I asked Amelia.

'I was, but Tilda rang and asked me to come for the horse-ride – she needs some moral support. I saw Fraser at an outside pub table and convinced him to join in.'

'Couldn't imagine anything more pleasurable than a horse-ride with a bunch of toffs.' Fraser shrugged.

'Ever been on a horse, Fraser?'

'Nope. How hard could it be? If Donald Pinstripe Crabshaw can do it, anybody can.'

Sam appeared. 'Ready for a ride guys? Fresh air, countryside, couldn't be better.'

'You sound chipper,' I commented.

'I am. Tilda and I had a long talk and I understand her better now. She's the woman for me – and we will be very happy again in South Beach away from all these...' Sam gestured to the group checking fit sizes for their helmets. 'Never ridden a horse in my life but how hard can it be? Grab a helmet, guys.'

Fraser and I reluctantly walked to the helmet basket.

'Talk to your horse, Fraser, bond with it,' yelled Sam as his horse bolted off with him clinging to the reins for dear life.

'Mine won't move!' Fraser bellowed at me. 'What's wrong with it? Come on horse, go.' Fraser's horse lowered its head to feed on the grass.

'Give him a gentle tap on the side with your leg,' Jordan Sticks shouted. 'That will get him going.'

'Fuck me,' Fraser yelled as his horse decided to take the tap seriously and raced after Sam's.

Jordan Sticks' horse and mine seemed to have a crush on each other and were reluctant to do anything other than trot together.

'You've obviously ridden a horse before,' I commented.

'Yes, it's the way I like to wind down from training – helps me de-stress. We've got our biggest game of the season coming up in a couple of weeks – against Bellbargo. We're getting a lot of pressure from the top to win this one and keep the investors happy.'

'The perils of professional sport.'

'Yes. I do yoga every day to keep my body flexible and able to handle the strain of matches. One injury and you're out. The stakes are too high for a club to support an injured player. Actually, Tilda and I used to ride a lot together when we were younger. She was older than me though – always looked out for me like a sister would. I missed her when she moved to South Beach. She still follows my career and calls me after big wins or losses. That Sam is a lucky guy. I wish I had someone serious in my life – every girl I meet is just interested in becoming a WAG and hanging out with the other wives and girlfriends on tours. I want more than a handbag relationship. I want a partner who has her own life and career and isn't dependent on me for her satisfaction and happiness. Having said that, what do you think of Polly? A good bit of entertainment during a drought?'

This could get awkward. 'Seems nice.' I was never one to kiss and tell. Jordan Sticks could have the pleasure of discovering Polly's quirks on his own.

Not surprisingly, Amelia directed her horse towards ours so she could flirt with Jordan. When we were on our own, I suggested, 'You're a bit hypocritical, aren't you – flirting with a younger guy?'

'He's out of his twenties.'

'True.'

'What's the story with Norrie? Why are we all out here on a horse-ride while he's lying dead at The Pied? Seems a little odd.' Amelia looked confused.

'It's what Tilda wanted, isn't it?' I asked.

'Yes. She's just bounced back remarkably fast – she was pretty upset this morning.'

'She probably hadn't seen Norrie for a long time up till a few days ago.'

'He did drool all over me at the picnic – I think Uncle Norrie may have passed his heyday. Still, I kind of wished I'd flirted with him a bit now – given him a good time before he carked it.'

'Really?'

'No. But sounds good in theory.'

'Bloody heck, look at Fraser.' I pointed. His horse had gone into the stream for a swim and Fraser was being dragged through the water, still clinging on.

The rest of the group followed Tilda to a clumping of Douglas fir trees and dismounted for a round of lemonades that Juliette and Clarence provided.

Several minutes later, a wet-looking Fraser came up to me and whispered, 'Mate, this has turned out to be a shitty holiday, hasn't it? I'm chafing where no man wants to chafe.'

'Ouch.'

My phone rang; it was Sinclair. Today was the day Glasward-Sade Hart was going to become a public company and he was calling with a progress report. I had to answer it.

Chapter 11

'All ducks are aligned for the listing,' Sinclair assured me. 'We've placed the thirty percent with Goldman's clients and we'll wait and watch what happens when the market opens.' He sounded keen. 'With your and Sandra's reputation, I'd say you'll definitely hit your seven-dollar-fifty per share target. This thing could fly a lot higher though. You may be about to become a very wealthy man.'

That was not the worst news I'd heard.

After relaying the conversation to Sandra, I re-joined the group under the fir trees. Sam was making a toast. 'Some of you may be wondering why we are out here after what happened to poor Uncle Norrie. Tilda wanted us to ride since it was one of Norrie's favourite activities – he was happiest out in the country air.'

'When not drunk,' Veda interjected.

'Anyway, I would like us all to raise our glasses to Uncle Norrie.'

'To Uncle Norrie.'

Ching.

'Do you really think he had a heart attack?' Samrina whispered to me.

'Huh?'

'It's just that I read a newspaper article about an old guy who died and everyone assumed it was his heart because of his age and lifestyle but actually he'd been murdered for an inheritance he was about to redirect.'

'Samrina, I think your imagination may be running away on you,' Sanjay interjected.

'You're probably right. Who would want to murder Norrie anyway? He seemed innocuous enough.'

'Who's been murdered?' Clarence pushed into the group.

'No one,' Sanjay awkwardly replied. 'We were just talking about a TV series.'

'Oh good. We wouldn't want a murder around here now, would we? That wouldn't be good for business – worse than the current situation of having Norrie's dead body in my hotel.'

'When are they planning on moving him?' Sanjay asked.

'I don't know. Norrie's two sisters are fighting over that right now.'

'Some cultures keep dead bodies in the house for days, sometimes weeks, to allow people enough time to be with the body and grieve in their own way,' Sanjay said. 'Morgues are only a recent invention in the path of history.'

'I know, but between you and me I do wish it wasn't my hotel he died in!' Clarence was flustered. 'Lord, look at Donald Crabshaw over there, busy on his phone. He must be under a lot of pressure right now – puts on a good external show but his world is crumbling around him.'

'How's that?' I glanced towards the pinstriped jodhpurs.

'Donald worked as an analyst at Morgans for the first half of his career and did very well. He then probably got a bit big for his boots because he decided to become a hedge fund manager. He has – or rather, had – a circle of very wealthy friends and relations so was quickly able to gather a large pool of funds to invest. He was the man about town for quite a few years. One year he produced a fifty percent return for his clients. He was the golden boy of investing who could do no wrong.

'This was the period after the global financial crisis when being bearish paid off and he was able to find some good opportunities to borrow shares and sell them at a high price on the market, betting the price would fall – at which point he would buy back the shares, return them to the loaner and happily soak up the profits.'

'I think I know how this story is going to play out,' I said.

'Yes. Unfortunately Donald never changed his investment strategy and has continued to believe in impending doom in the sharemarket. He has consistently taken short positions on stocks in the hope that the share prices will fall. This behaviour has hurt him several times and he's lost a lot of money for his clients. Every fund manager can have a bad year, so at first his clients gave him the benefit of the doubt, but four years of consecutive bad returns and his friends can no longer remain loyal. They are exiting his fund and taking their money elsewhere.

'It's a very awkward situation. Juliette and I lost money with him, so did Sanjay and Samrina here, Barbara and Veda, and poor old Norrie. Norrie would have died knowing he didn't have much left to his name at all.'

'And Jordan Sticks,' Sanjay added. 'Donald Crabshaw also had some of his money to invest, amongst others.'

'It makes things difficult for us all being here,' Samrina admitted. 'He's a nice enough guy, I guess, but he just read the market and economic situation so badly. Truthfully, I feel mad whenever I see him.'

'Jamieson, you know how hard investing can be. Donald's definitely had a bad run.' Clarence put his hands in his pockets and started nudging a stone on the ground with his foot.

'The problem is –' Veda pushed into the group '– Donald bloody Crabshaw still walks around in his pinstriped suits with his phone to his ear, acting all superior to the rest of us, when he has drained a lot of our wealth. I was planning on buying an estate near here. Turn it into an organic farm and hold yoga and meditation retreats. I don't think I'll be able to do that now, thanks to Donald. I spend a lot of time wishing I'd never met that guy and just kept my money in the bank.'

'Oh, come on now, Veda,' Clarence protested. 'You know you would have only got two-percent from the bank. Equities can provide excellent returns in the long run.'

'It depends who you're invested with though, doesn't it? I saw some of the crazy bets Donald was taking with our money and thought, *What is he doing, I could do a better job than this!*'

I had to respond here. 'Every fund manager's clients feel that way at different times. It happens with some of our clients – they'll hear a rumour about a company, a half-story perhaps, and will make up the rest of the story in their heads, then come to me demanding we sell their shares. The problem is, these rumours are generally unfounded, and selling the shares can unnecessarily tilt the balance of their portfolios. Sometimes a company can experience a rough patch but we stay invested in order to realise the longer-term gains. Knee-jerk reactions don't help anyone in this business.'

'Your investment record is outstanding – over twenty years, Jamieson.' Clarence stroked my ego. 'You clearly know what you're doing.'

'Are we talking about Donald Crabshaw?' Barbara butted in.

'As a matter of fact, yes,' replied Clarence.

'Good. It's about time someone talked about the elephant in the room – or should I say meadow?'

Donald was still out of earshot on his phone call.

'We're all too British to say anything, aren't we? God save the queen and all that.' Barbara hauled down her shirt that had ridden up over the top of her pants, and I noticed she was wearing two Union Jack pins. 'Talking about money is dreadfully common but I am too old to be losing the amounts he lost for me. I'm going to have to sell one of my weekend properties – Sandringham or Balmoral. I'm not sure which one I can bear to part with. And all because of the actions of that scoundrel!'

Investing was tough and the stakes were high, something fund managers were reminded of every day. Donald Crabshaw wouldn't have deliberately made these losses. Perhaps he could've had a more diverse portfolio, I wondered. He had tried to beat the market and lost. Sometimes high absolute returns need to be enough instead of constantly trying to chase relative ones.

'I wonder who invests the royal family's money – I bet they don't make a mess of it like Donald has.'

Barbara really was a royal fanatic. I pointed out, 'They will have years of poor performance and years of outperformance like everybody else.'

'Are you defending Donald?' Barbara snapped.

'Not entirely – he's clearly had a rough ride. I'm just saying that next year is a new year, I have no idea about Donald's investment philosophy other than that he may have been too conservative. I really am unable to comment.'

'Sanjay and I will have to work for a few years longer than we would've liked to recover our losses.' Samrina didn't look thrilled with the prospect.

'At least you are young.' Barbara was not going to let this go. 'I'm old – I don't have time to wait for my investments to recover. I must make decisions now.'

'Finally we have found something we agree on Barbara.' Veda gently squeezed Barbara's arm. 'It really is an awful situation to be in. Jordan Sticks over there–' Jordan was talking to Amelia by the horses '–was invested with Donald too but he doesn't look too sad about it. I'm guessing that with his soccer career earning him millions a year he doesn't have too much to worry about.'

Chapter 12

I'd had enough of mixing with that lot so mounted my horse, left the group and explored the countryside. It was a predominantly rural landscape, the lush green meadows divided by thick stone walls into what appeared to be hobby farms. Wheat seemed to be the most popular crop – in this region anyway.

A group of walkers dressed in camouflage gear and carrying cameras appeared at the brow of a hill. They walked towards me, yelling 'Get the horse out of here. Hurry up, move on.'

'Excuse me, is there a problem?' I looked down from the horse.

'There jolly well is,' replied a bald, older man, trying to untangle his camera strap from a bird whistle. 'We're trying to find a very rare bird that was last sighted in this region a few days ago. It's not going to land anywhere with a ruddy great horse plodding about, is it?'

There were about thirty birdwatchers in the group, furious with my supposed trespass. I wasn't in the mood for confrontation so turned my horse and cantered back towards The Pied. All I could think was, it was a shame Polly had turned out to be so annoying – I really could have done with some female company. I'm not a prude in the boudoir by any means; I just don't get off on props and food. Nudity, desire and lack of inhibition is all it takes, from both partners.

Juliette was brushing the horses outside the small stable to the back of The Pied when I returned.

'Hello, Jamieson. Did you enjoy your ride?'

'Yes, until I was forced to turn around by a group of bird watchers.'

'Ah, you ran into some twitchers, did you? They've been getting excited and descending here in hordes ever since someone spotted a rare blue thrush. Apparently fifteen hundred twitchers have been through Chipping Norton – the village near here – in the past week. They must have spread their wings, excuse the pun, to Avon-On-The-Water. Curious folk, I always think. They spend so much time sitting in silence, waiting for the flash of a view of one of these rare creatures. I get my kicks other ways.'

'Which ways would they be?'

'I like sky-diving.'

'Really? Can you do it around here?'

'Yes, there's a business operating on an old airfield about twenty miles away. They take you up and you jump. Can't get enough of it myself although Clarence isn't so keen.'

'I don't blame him.'

'You'd enjoy it, you feel free as a bird up there. Even Donald Crabshaw enjoyed it – we used to date before I met Clarence. I tandem skydived with him a few times but Clarence? I can't even get him up for the flight let alone a jump.'

'Small world, huh? You dating Donald before Clarence.'

'Yes, you could say I don't have much range – went from a hedge fund manager to an investment banker. But then again, I was in investor relations myself so I was unlikely to marry a playwright or any other person with a non-finance job, I guess. I was so happy the day Clarence suggested we buy this place. Don't get me wrong, it's hard work, but any work is made a lot easier with this view.'

'I couldn't argue with that.'

'We'll be setting up out here tonight for Tilda and Sam's vow renewals tomorrow morning. It'll be an early start for us all since Tilda wants the service to be held at sunrise. Dawn is a beautiful time of the day here – the sun rises just over those hills through there. Our rooster likes it too – I guess you've heard him. He starts up at 6am – likes to compete with the church bells, I think. Sam and Tilda didn't want to renew their vows in a church. Nothing is more beautiful or spiritual than nature if you ask me.'

I nodded, then excused myself to answer the call I'd been waiting on from Sinclair.

'Glasward-Sade Hart is listed. Opening price was seven-dollars-fifty but it has since risen to seven-eighty a share – no, eight-twenty as we speak. Congratulations, Jamieson. I'm guessing you will be celebrating this new windfall in style?'

'When I get back to South Beach I will be – this trip has been ho-hum to say the least.'

I then called Sandra.

'Jamieson, great news! This will help me out of my bind with money to spare, and we still own seventy percent of the company. I hope you're as happy as I am?'

'Sure am. I should tell you now that I am thinking about resigning as chief investment officer and taking a seat on the board.'

'Huh?'

'Kenneth Chow is keen to partner me on buying Xtrapak and setting it up as an investment company. Any profits made through Xtrapak will be fed directly into new opportunities – for want of a better word, it will be my Berkshire Hathaway. I can't do that at the same time as investing for Glasward-Sade Hart.'

'Why not?'

'Well, I could, but it would create a conflict of interest between the two companies.'

'Not as I see it. To tell you the truth, some of the private-equity-type behaviour you indulge in with smaller companies gives me the wobbles. I would be happy for you to run a big-cap portfolio for our clients, giving them the option to invest in Xtrapak and whatever other opportunity rears its head with Kenneth.'

This conversation was going better than I'd imagined. 'That is possible, I guess.'

'I could market it beautifully to our clients – a new, small, very active equity product run and invested in by Jamieson Hart. Many of our clients have been asking me if they could mirror your own portfolio and this gives them the chance. Who knows, when I get back on my feet financially I may even invest in you.' Sandra laughed.

'Sandra, you have made me a very happy man. I'm keen to get this investment company idea with Kenneth Chow off the ground but I would have found it hard to walk away from my role in Glasward-Sade Hart.'

'Let's always keep talking, huh? Never run off and make rash decisions without me – I may be more biddable than you think.'

Chapter 13

I went to the bar and bought beers for Sam and Fraser, and a Bacardi and Coke for myself. Sam and Fraser were seated at an outdoor table with a friendly cat trying to gain their attention.

'Thanks, mate. What are we celebrating?' Fraser asked as I handed them their drinks.

'Apart from the obvious,' Sam pointed out.

'Yes, of course – sorry, Sam. Apart from the bloody vow renewal thing, what are we celebrating? Please tell me it's something good.' Fraser took a sip of his beer.

Sam had his hand in a bowl of chips and shrugged like it wasn't worth getting offended.

'Sandra and I are selling a stake in Glasward-Sade Hart and so far it's going well.'

'Oh, mate, does this mean I should finally figure out what it is you do?' Fraser looked disappointed. 'I know you choose shares in companies for your clients to buy but not much more than that.'

'That's all you need to know.'

'Congratulations!' Sam tried to avoid us seeing his mouthful of chips.

'Does this mean you will now be even more loaded and will move to an even bigger house in South Beach?' Fraser asked.

'Never. My bachelor pad suits me just fine – and living next door to my kids makes it perfect.'

'And we keep you grounded. You know Sam and I aren't into you for your money.'

'Keep drinking, Fraser. I know that.'

'So, I'm getting married again tomorrow.' Sam changed the topic. 'Feel more nervous this time than I did ten years ago.'

'Why's that?' I asked.

'Tilda and I know each other so much better now. At the first ceremony, we were both young and dumb, and happy to throw caution to the wind. This time I know she'll be up all night tonight ruminating on whether we are suited for each other – and who's to say she'll actually turn up tomorrow? I'm too old to be left standing at the altar.'

'Remind us again why we trekked across the globe to be here, Sam?' Fraser put his head in his hand.

'At least you got a free flight from it, Fray.' Sam was trying to be upbeat.

'At least I got to meet Lucy, I guess – who is waiting for me in London, I might add, so once your nuptials are over I'm heading back down there to renew our acquaintance.'

Tilda arrived at the table. 'Jamieson, I don't trust Fraser, but can I count on you to keep Sam sober so he's at his best tomorrow morning? We will be up with the larks.'

I looked at Sam. There was no way. 'Absolutely,' I replied.

'Good I have got so much to do. The bunting has started to detach itself from the oaks, the lectern hasn't arrived yet, and I have a last-minute dressmaker about to arrive to take the bust in on my dress – it appears I have lost weight in that area in the last few days.'

'Your day keeps getting better, doesn't it, Sam?' Fraser patted him on the back.

My phone rang. To my surprise it was Sinclair again – it was unusual for him to call back so quickly.

'Jamieson, I don't know how to put his but I have some bad news. I've heard via the blasted rumour mill here that two guys are quickly buying shares in Glasward-Sade Hart and are talking about getting over the five percent threshold, then calling a meeting to vote for a seat on the board.'

'*What?* Who would do that?'

'Their names are Frank D'Arcy and Corrin Smales.'

'Fuck.'

'Who are they?'

'It was a deal I did before your time, Sinclair, in the early days. I ousted the CEO and chairman of a board – it was hostile, you might say.'

'D'Arcy and Smales?'

'I knew I'd paid them way too much when they left.'

'And now they're using it to seek revenge.'

'It appears so. How much have they got?'

'Four-point-five percent combined. We can't stop this – they will get to five if that's what they're wanting. In fact, I can see it on my screen now, they're at five percent. They've met the threshold and can now call a shareholder meeting to put up the vote.'

'I need a list of the other shareholders – I have to figure out who my friends and enemies are before this vote takes place.'

'Absolutely. I'll email it. I'm sorry this has happened to you... is that a sheep I hear now?'

'Yes, and this stupid trip to England has to come to an end. I'll try and get a flight out tomorrow afternoon.' I closed my phone. Frank D'Arcy and Corrin Smales. Bastards.

I called Sandra, and discovered she'd already seen their names come up.

'Jamieson, what's going on with the share register? Why have D'Arcy and Smale's names appeared? It's like reliving a nightmare.'

'It's worse than reliving a nightmare – D'Arcy and Smales are gunning for us. Actually, I don't know about you but they're definitely coming for me. Word has it they're going to call a shareholders' meeting to get a seat on the board so they can make the running of the firm very difficult.'

'That's not going to happen. We are smarter at this game than they are and those two need to realise that.'

'Hold on a minute, Sandra.' A message had come through on my phone. 'Just heard from Sinclair – they've lodged notice for a meeting in two days' time.

He has sent through a list of the shareholders. No doubt D'Arcy and Smales will be on the phone drumming up support.'

'So will I. I'll work the phones day and night to determine our level of support. I am sorry about this, Jamieson. If we hadn't have listed, these sharks wouldn't have had the opportunity to attack us.'

'Don't be sorry – we're not done yet. Work that share register and get us a majority vote. I have a plan for finishing business with D'Arcy and Smales for good afterwards. They want to come at me? Let them. I can handle this.'

Chapter 14

When I returned to the others, Tilda had obviously left to go and get her dress fixed and whatever else was of excruciating importance.

'Bad phone call?' Sam asked.

'Yes, actually. As we speak, two guys are set on trying to make life difficult at Glasward-Sade Hart.'

'Jeepers,' was Sam's response. 'Why?'

'It's a revenge move from two guys I sacked several years ago. It seems they saw our listing and took their chance.'

'Yours was a private firm. Why did you think it would be a good idea to sell shares to strangers?' Fraser asked.

'Sandra needed the cash – and truthfully, in theory it should have worked out well for me because I'm going to use the cash to fund a new business with a Singaporean business partner while continuing to be CIO of Glasward-Sade Hart. Listings can be excellent ways to raise equity when you need it, as long as you aren't burdened with hostile shareholders.'

'Like in this instance,' said Fraser.

'Yes, I clearly didn't hit the jackpot in terms of investors. I need another drink. Anyone else?'

'You don't want to work on this?' Sam asked.

'There's nothing I can do at this point – Sandra is working the register. I'm pretty sure I'll get through the vote okay, and I've already formulated an idea of how to get rid of these turkeys for good once the vote is through.'

'How are you going to do that?' Fraser asked.

'I'm going to short my own company.'

'Huh? I have no idea what that means.'

'I'll explain it when it happens. How about that drink?'

'I need one too.' Sam sensed I was happy for a topic change.

'You were supposed to stay sober for Tilda.' For the first time this trip, Fraser was trying to be helpful.

'Nah, I need to drink to get through this and Jamieson clearly needs some help.'

I was already on my way to the bar. 'Bacardi and Coke, and two of your best local craft beers, thanks.'

Somewhat annoyingly we were joined by Sanjay and Samrina.

'We're looking forward to the ceremony tomorrow, Sam,' Sanjay told him. 'Then we're out of here, back to London to keep saving for a new house we have our hearts set on – the one we're in at the moment was really only meant to be temporary. Did you see the write-up on what Christopher Bond, the multimillionaire media mogul, had to say on the housing market? He reckons people these days can't afford decent houses because we spend too much on lattes and eating out.'

'That's codswallop and makes me so angry.' Samrina's face turned pink. 'I am sick of multimillionaires telling me why I can't afford a new house. Housing prices are higher than they've ever been, pushed up largely by the likes of Christopher investing in property. At the same time rents are high, which makes saving for a deposit even harder for people who aren't like Sanjay and me, already owning a home. The average rate of savings for the younger generation is higher than it's been since the seventies. I don't know any person trying to buy a house who flippantly spends without assessing the consequences. Being lectured to by someone who's part of the cause of the housing problem does not sit well with me. To say the least. Of course we would have been a lot better off it weren't for Donald Crabshaw over there.' Samrina gestured at Donald, who was leant against the bar, cradling a red wine. 'He got so caught up in the heady glamour of being wined and dined by brokers he never did thorough due diligence on any investment.'

'Oh, well, we already have eighty-five percent of the cash required for the new place,' Sanjay comforted her. 'A few more years and we'll be ready to buy. We just don't want to borrow, be tied down by a mortgage.'

Any sympathy I had for these two had dwindled. They were fine. Donald had made some mistakes, but, as far as I could tell, none of his clients were anywhere near the breadline. I had problems of my own and wasn't prepared to entertain theirs any longer. Fortunately when they'd finished their drink they left.

Fraser looked towards the stables. 'I think that guy, Jordan Sticks, is the only one having any fun around here.'

Polly was pinned against the stable wall and Jordan had one hand on the wall holding his weight, the other hand flicking her hair as he was about to go in for a kiss.

'The only one having a good time around here? Thanks, Fraser.' Sam was not happy.

'Sorry, Sam.'

'No, I mean it, Fraser. I am sick of you whinging – that's all you've done since you got here. Maybe you should have stayed in London with whoever the heck she was…actually, I don't know why I even asked you to come here.'

Fraser looked guilty and Sam slunk down on the table. 'Oh, no, I'm so sorry, Fraser. I didn't mean any of it. The whole atmosphere is getting to me. I just want this ceremony over and then I'm heading home to South Beach, back to Café Tropicana and the beach and the tennis club.'

I couldn't agree with him more. I couldn't wait to squeeze my kids and get back to my bachelor pad, hear the sound of lorikeets, watch the palm fronds sway in the breeze – and get away from these whingeing guests who actually didn't have much to whinge about.

'It's okay, Sam, I deserve some of what you said. I haven't exactly been the life of the party. I just feel out of my league here and it makes me uncomfortable. I'm not a banker or snobby fund manager – sorry, Jamieson – or a management consultant, or a receiver of a large inheritance. I'm just a detective from South Beach, and I like it that way. Here, though, I'm a fish out of water.'

'Here's to South Beach, vow renewals and getting out of here.' Sam raised his glass.

'To getting out of here,' Fraser and I chorused.

Chapter 15

My alarm rang at 5am – the same time as the church bells. The rooster had yet to awaken. My feet put themselves on the floor and walked my body to the bathroom. It was the morning we had all been hauled here for.

Showered and wearing a suit, I headed over to the oaks. Amelia was wearing a rose-coloured silk dress that stuck to her like liquid; she was simply stunning.

'Good morning. You are beautiful.'

'Thank you. You look dapper yourself.'

'Why is it that we broke up again?'

'I have a list of reasons. Do you want to hear them?'

'No, but out of everyone here today, I know for sure that you are the one person I want to talk to most.'

'That's actually very sweet.'

'Let's take a seat under that bough. When the sun does rise it will shield us from needing to squint.'

'You look like you didn't get much sleep last night.'

'I didn't.'

'Problems at work?'

'Yes, actually. If Frank D'Arcy and Corrin Smales have their way, life at Glasward-Sade Hart will be very difficult as of tomorrow.'

'I remember those names – from back in the day when we were still together. Arseholes, weren't they? Totally incapable idiots who screwed the company they were at for a massive redundancy package when really they'd been fired.'

I loved the way Amelia didn't choose to soften the edges. 'That's right.'

'How interested does that make you in sitting though this farcical ceremony?'

'Not very, but I'm glad to have you by my side. Besides, I'm booked to get out of here after the ceremony.'

'We might not be suited being married but I still like you, you know.'

That was all I needed to hear as Amelia and I went to take our seats next to Fraser.

'Look at Sam – he's sweating.' I observed.

He was standing at the front of the short aisle, rocking from foot to foot. The man needed to wipe his brow, and wet marks were appearing on his shirt. I hoped Tilda didn't keep him waiting.

'We're all here –' Barbara had come down the aisle to check '– except for Jordan Sticks. Does anyone know where he is?'

No one replied.

'Well, he's twenty minutes late and the bride is waiting. I will tell her to start the ceremony – we can't sit around waiting for him to be bothered to turn up. You'd think he'd be used to early mornings, for goodness' sake, with all the soccer training he does.'

'I think he's getting a bit of training in with Polly,' I whispered to Amelia.

'What?'

'I saw them kissing by the stables last night.'

'He's gone down in the world, in my opinion, to choose a woman like Polly.'

'As opposed to a woman like you?'

'Exactly.'

The music started and Sam looked relieved to see Tilda appear. I admit Tilda did look hot – she had gone for a very exposed cleavage and Sam embarrassed himself by being unable to look at anything else.

The ceremony proceeded as expected – Sam said 'I do', then Tilda said 'I do', and that was it. Time for a wedding brunch, then I'd be packing my bags and on the afternoon flight.

My train of thought was interrupted by an almighty *bang* followed by 'Help! Someone help!' It was Polly's voice. 'Jordan's bleeding and all messed up. Quick, someone help – please!'

Polly was stumbling towards us whilst trying to support Jordan who then collapsed on her. Clarence pulled out his phone and called an ambulance. Juliette was the first to reach them, and helped Polly lower Jordan gently to the grass.

'What happened?' Juliette asked Polly.

'I don't know, it was all so awful. Jordan stepped out of his room to come to the wedding. He was running late because we'd been shagging –' the woman had no filtering system '– and something exploded on him!'

I followed Fraser to the entrance of Jordan's room, which was just out of sight of the ceremony venue.

'It's a bomb!' Fraser was picking though the pieces on the ground. 'Someone has placed a bomb here to explode – I guess when Jordan opened his door. This is attempted murder.' Fraser looked me in the eye. 'Neither of us will be getting out of here today, Jamieson. This is a homicide case and the local police will want to speak to all of us.'

Fraser stayed by the door, securing the scene, and called the local police. The rest of the guests were huddled around Jordan.

Tilda was on the ground beside him, saying, 'Come on, Jordan, stay with me. You're not going anywhere. Stay with me, that's it, keep your eyes open, stay with me, Jordan, stay with me!' Juliette had run inside The Pied and grabbed bandages and was wrapping them around the injuries to Jordan's legs.

Barbara was hyperventilating. 'I can't stand blood, I can't – it makes me sick. Oh no, I think I'm going to be sick. I don't want to disgrace myself but I'm going to be sick.'

'Barbara, go inside – you're no help to anyone like this.' Veda was right.

Donald Crabshaw was awkwardly trying to help but really doing nothing other than getting in the way, and Sanjay was holding Samrina who was clearly squeamish.

Amelia whispered to me, 'What happened?'

'It looks like he triggered a bomb when he stepped outside his door.'

'What the hell? He did *what?*'

'I know. It was some kind of explosive device but I don't know how it all happened – Fraser is waiting for the local police to arrive.'

'I cannot comprehend that. We are in this quaint village on the other side of the world, there is nothing offensive around here – just sheep for goodness' sake – and someone plants a bomb to blow up Jordan Sticks?'

'It appears so.'

'Why?'

'I have no idea.'

Sirens cut through the silence of the countryside and soon paramedics arrived and were bent down over Jordan before lifting him up onto a stretcher and transporting him to the ambulance. At least he was alive.

'Jamieson, I want to get out of here.' Amelia looked scared. 'Who else is going to be hit by a bomb? Is it a terrorist who did this?'

'I doubt it. It was clearly targeted at Jordan Sticks. A terrorist would have gone for all of us at the ceremony, wouldn't they? Or the shops on the main strip.'

'I guess so.'

'It doesn't sound sympathetic, I know, but my biggest problem right now is that I'm not going to be able to catch the afternoon flight from Heathrow. We have now got ourselves involved in an attempted murder scene.'

'Oh, my goodness, I can't believe all this. I'm going to call the kids and tell them how much I love them. I'll tell my folks not to let the kids know what has just happened — I don't want them worrying about both their parents. I just remembered too that

Norrie's body is still in a room here. Aargh, what's wrong with this place? A dead body lying around and now someone gets hit by a bomb?'

'It is a little out of the ordinary.'

'You reckon?' Amelia opened her phone and walked over to the stables.

Again, sirens pierced the air as several police cars pulled up on the gravel driveway. A news reporter arrived at the same time – word had travelled fast that Jordan Sticks from Ramlock United had been the target of a bombing. Several police officers cordoned off the crime scene and members of the bomb squad started analysing the parts that remained.

Chapter 16

Clarence called out to the guests, 'This is quite a shock to everyone. I suggest we all move inside to the pub. I'll close it off to the rest of the public. You all must be hungry so breakfast is on The Pied.'

Once inside, Samrina, who was wearing a purple and gold sari, said, 'Thank heavens Jordan is okay. Why is the bomb squad here? What on earth is going on?'

Fraser had appeared through the side door. 'The bomb squad is here because Jordan was hit with an explosive device.'

'How do you know?' Samrina started shaking.

'I am a detective in the South Beach police force. I have seen many explosive devices in my time.'

Tilda started crying. 'Who would want to hurt Jordan? He was a little brother to me.'

'Still is, darling.' Sam held her. 'Jordan is still alive.'

'This is all my fault. Why did I decide to come here for our vow renewals? We could have gone anywhere. Someone must have found out Jordan was staying here. I should have arranged security – he's so well known. Who would have wanted to do this to him?' Tilda's mascara ran down her cheeks.

'Some fans can become obsessive and stalkerish. This is potentially the work of a deranged fan,' Donald Crabshaw offered. 'It happens, you know. Remember the tennis player years ago who was attacked on court at the US Open by a knife-wielding fan? Sometimes it can be the ultimate price to pay for being famous.'

'Clear off!' Juliette yelled as she pulled the curtains to block a photographer who'd arrived and was taking photos though the windows. She turned to Clarence. 'This is private property - surely we can get rid of them?'

'We certainly can.' Clarence stormed out to have a go at the reporters.

'This is the last kind of publicity we need.' Juliette shook her head. 'An attempted murder on a famous soccer player. And I can just imagine how the press will react if they find out Norrie's body is still in room twenty-six!'

'That is a ridiculous situation,' Barbara agreed, and turned towards Veda. 'Are you happy now? Norrice should have been in a morgue. How are we going to get him out of here, with the place crawling in reporters?'

'I wasn't to know someone would try and murder Jordan! Norrie is peaceful, so maybe he'll need to stay here until this all dies down. Sorry, not a very good choice in words.'

'How do we know Norrie wasn't murdered too?' Smarina asked.

'Be quiet, you silly girl.' Barbara was sharp. 'No one would want to murder anyone in my family. Upstanding citizens we all are.' Barbara pulled the sides of her jacket then wiped imaginary lint form the lapels.

'She has a point, Barbara.' A concerned expression grew on Veda's face. 'I think the police need to be told about this.'

'The police? Are you mad, woman? Our brother Norrice died of a heart attack, simple as that. He must be allowed to rest in peace.'

At this point Fraser interjected, 'I'm sorry, Barbara, but I agree with Veda. I have already told the police about Norrie and I expect a hearse here very soon, to take his body for autopsy.'

'Isn't that brilliant – our brother hauled out of here under the eyes of paparazzi. What a scandal for the family!'

'It isn't a scandal, Barbara.'

'Really, Veda? I can just see the headline, "Norrice Rothman murdered as well as the attempted murder of Jordan Sticks!" Everyone will start asking what they did to deserve it. It will cast a very dark cloud over the family.'

'I don't think people generally conclude it is the fault of the victim when someone is murdered.' Sanjay was a reasonable guy.

'Can everyone please stop saying the word murder!' Tilda yelled. 'I just can't take any more of this talk.'

The door opened and Clarence appeared. 'I would be surprised if any reporter dares step on our property,' he declared. 'They just got a verbal lashing from me.' He eyed the basket of croissants that had been brought out by one of the kitchen staff. 'Ah, now I'm sure we'll all feel better with some food. Help yourselves, everyone. Tea and coffee are on the way.'

'I don't feel like eating when an explosive has just gone off around here.' Samrina picked at her croissant.

'It is all a bit unpalatable, isn't it?' Donald Crabshaw took a large bite of his.

'If anyone were to be murdered, it should be you, Donald.' Barbara was fierce.

'Barbara, stop.' Veda touched her sister on the arm.

'No, I won't stop. I will say what we all think. It should have been you, Donald – you're the one who has changed the lives of most of us here.'

'Who the hell do you think you are, Barbara?' Samrina snapped. 'He hasn't changed your life much. Anyway, it's your generation buying investment properties that have kept upward pressure on housing prices –'

'And the Russians and Ukrainians,' Clarence interrupted.

Samrina ignored that. 'So now Sanjay and I have to wait a few more years to afford to buy what we want. Yes, Donald lost some of our money, but your generation is to blame for the situation many younger people are in who simply cannot afford to buy a house.'

'You have no idea what you are talking about.' Barbara raised her voice. 'My husband and I worked very hard for everything we had that wasn't covered by inheritances. I ensure all our rental flats are maintained to a very high standard so that the occupiers feel proud to live where they do.'

'And then you sit back, collecting the income, while laughing in one of your three estates, no doubt.' Samrina wasn't going to let this go.

'How rude you are.'

Veda pointed out, 'We did have it very easy, Barbara.'

'What are you talking about?'

'We inherited a lot.'

'Yes, well, you may have wasted yours on organics and yoga and all those other fringe things you do that I try to keep quiet from my friends, but William and I invested soundly.'

'In the property market!' Samrina yelled.

'Excuse me, Barbara.' Veda's eyes narrowed. 'I am sick and tired of being the sister you barely acknowledge. I am doing more good in this world than you could ever dream of. The pesticides on fruit and vegetables are toxic, and the flow-on effects to humans and animals are alarming. People are so caught up in their lives they forget to live. Our retreats return them to themselves and make them realise what life is all about.'

'See, total codswallop. Who needs to be returned to themselves? Utterly pointless. I guess every family has an oddball in it.'

'You are being totally offensive. I have to believe it is a result of the situation we're in,' Veda replied. 'I'm not going to hurt myself by giving any power to what you have just said. I will let the words float past me.'

'That and any good idea you may have had during a lifetime.'

'Ladies, keep it together, please. This has become quite a show.' Donald Crabshaw was enjoying the moment.

'Shut up, Donald,' Barbara and Veda said in unison.

Barbara sighed loudly. 'This is awful. We need a prayer. A prayer for Norrice and Jordan Sticks, and hope that our family will be unaffected by the news broadcast. Sanjay, you're religious – lead us in prayer please.'

'I am not religious. I study and lecture in religion but I am not religious.'

Barbara flung her hands in the air. 'For goodness' sake, it's like making cakes but hating sponge.'

'How about we all just take a break?' Clarence tried to settle everyone. 'The police will be in here soon to ask questions.'

'Of course, we're all suspects.' Barbara's voice oozed sarcasm. 'Forget the idea that a lunatic fan ran in off the street and planted a bomb for Jordan – it was me, I kept the bomb in the back of my Mercedes all along. How ludicrous.' She propped up her oversized glasses and stalked over to the corner of the room to take a seat.

'I'm really struggling with that word bomb,' Samrina said as she and Sanjay sat by the fire, which needed to burn since it felt like ten degrees Celsius despite it being early summer.

'Oh, well, work to do. Busy busy, you know,' said Donald Crabshaw in his pinstripes. 'The global market never sleeps.' He took a seat by the window and opened his phone.

Clarence and Juliette tried to look busy behind the bar.

Tilda turned to Amelia and said, 'Can we talk? I need it.'

Amelia agreed and they sat at the end of the bar on stools.

That left one corner for Fraser, Sam and me.

Chapter 17

'Best wedding ever, mate.' Fraser tried to make light of the situation.

Sam groaned. 'Is it too early for a beer?'

My phone rang. Mirabelle. Reluctantly I answered.

'Oh, Mr Hart, I so pleased you answer. It is I, Mirabelle. I speak to Mrs Hart's mother –' Amelia's parents were getting too cosy with Mirabelle '– and she say someone explode with a bomb! Mr Hart, you have terrorist with you – you must go now.'

'No, Mirabelle, there is no terrorist. It was a famous soccer player who was attacked, possibly by an obsessed fan.'

'Oh, no, Mr Hart, that is not so. No fan has means to make bomb, and why make bomb? Fans attack with knife or gun, not bomb!'

I had to agree – a bomb did seem a little excessive. 'Regardless, we are quite safe here.'

'You silly silly man. You not safe. One man bombed, other man killed as well.'

'Tilda's uncle died of a heart attack.' I was convincing myself of this as much as Mirabelle.

'No, it is dark, Mr Hart, very dark.'

'Thank you, Mirabelle. Is there another reason why you were ringing?'

'No, Mr Hart.'

I thought as much.

'But –'

'Sorry, Mirabelle, I need to go. I will talk to you later.'

'Mr Hart –'

I closed my phone.

'It will be interesting to be on the receiving end of an interrogation.' Fraser signalled to the two police officers who had just entered the pub.

'Good morning, all. My name is Detective Sergeant Bill Rhodes and this is Detective John Pillcock. We are investigating the attempted murder of Jordan Sticks via an explosive device. We ask you all to remain in the village of Avon-On-The-Water until further notice.'

'There go my hopes with Lucy in London,' Fraser whispered.

'Now, we have a few questions we need to ask each of you,' the detective continued.

'I don't know what you would need to ask us,' Clarence said. 'We were all seated for Sam and Tilda's vow renewals until we heard a bang, and then Polly appeared trying to hold Jordan. It couldn't have been any of us. Actually, where is Polly?'

'I have already spoken to Ms Polly. She is now talking to a victim support person.'

'A victim support person? Are my taxes being paid for someone to comfort a murderer?'

Everyone looked at Donald Crabshaw.

'Well, if it wasn't some lunatic fan – who, quite frankly, nobody saw – then it must have been that Polly. She was the only one with Jordan. Obvious, isn't it? Why are the police comforting her?'

'We need to investigate this fully.'

'Well, you haven't got off to a rollicking start, have you?'

'Good one, Donald. Harass a police officer.' Juliette rolled her eyes at him.

'It doesn't take a rocket scientist to figure out who did it. I don't know why we need to waste our time.'

'The man talks sense occasionally.'

'Shut up, Barbara,' said Samrina.

'Right, so ... Donald Crabshaw, is it? Explain your movements this morning,' Bill started.

'I heard the cow mooing – that wakes me up each morning. Bloody thing, right outside my window. Then I showered, got dressed and walked over to the ceremony venue. I joined Veda on the way since she was exiting her room at the same time as me.'

'Veda?' the detective asked.

'Yes, that's me,' Veda confirmed. 'I heard footsteps on the gravel outside my room so I opened the door to join whomever was already on their way to the ceremony. No one was there, but Donald opened his door so I walked with him.'

'I heard footsteps too. They sounded like they were running,' Sanjay interjected.

'You didn't tell me this?' said Samrina.

'You were putting on your pearls, and I never assumed hearing someone running could be a sign of something sinister. Samrina and I left our room just after Veda and Donald, and we followed them to the ceremony.'

'There we go. Look on the CCTV camera and you'll find the mystery owner of the footsteps and we can all go home,' said Barbara.

'We don't have CCTV,' Clarence said.

'It's getting fitted next week,' Juliette explained.

'You are kidding me,' said Barbara.

'Unfortunately not.' Clarence rocked awkwardly from side to side.

'They don't add much value anyway,' Samrina supported Clarence. 'One of my management consulting jobs was with a security firm. The cameras act as a deterrent at best, but mostly criminals just cover their faces with a balaclava or the like so you can't tell who they are, and you can spend thousands monitoring the film. Waste of money, if you ask me.'

I had invested in a security company and disagreed with Samrina, but that discussion was for another time.

'Of course, you would say that – your knowledge on anything appears to be a mile wide and an inch deep,' Barbara retorted – clearly not over the accusation that she had been one of the parties to blame for the housing bubble.

The detective directed his eye towards me. 'Name, sir?'

'Jamieson Hart. I was woken by my alarm clock at 5am, showered, then walked outside to the ceremony.'

Fraser, Sam and Tilda all had the same story.

'Right, well, that's not getting us anywhere. As I said, please remain in the village while we continue our investigations.'

'What the hell is going on?' Sam looked at me and Fraser.

'I've got no idea.' Fraser reached for his croissant. 'If it were one of the guests they would have had to hide the device this whole time, but I guess – as that nutcase Barbara pointed out – they could have hidden it in the boot of their car. It could have been a fan but it's a pretty complex device to tuck under your jacket and run with. Still, stranger things have happened.'

'Take me back to when Tilda was having a midlife crisis and demanding sex to keep her young.' Sam gulped his beer. 'Instead, I imagine we're headed for couple's counselling when we get home.'

'Really? I thought you'd sorted things out,' I asked.

'So did I, but Tilda's been ruminating on it and this morning only agreed to remarry me if we went to couple's counselling.'

'I wonder how many other people have accepted a proposal on that condition?' Fraser couldn't contain his laughter.

'I'd say I'm the only lucky bastard,' said Sam.

Chapter 18

Amelia walked over to our table. 'Feel like coming down to the shops for a coffee?'

I certainly did. I knew from past experience Sam and Fraser would be sitting in the same place when I returned, having progressed not much further in the conversation.

The sun was surprisingly warm and our shoes made loud scratchy noises over the gravel. Sheep were grazing in the meadow along with the lone cow that clearly bothered Donald Crabshaw. The cicadas had kicked up a gear in the chorus, seemingly unaware of the police combing the crime scene or the paparazzi directing long-lens cameras at us and shouting questions.

'Do you know what happened to Jordan Sticks?'

'Do you have any comment?'

'Who died here? We saw the hearse.'

'No comment.' Thankfully they then left Amelia and me alone, cameras in wait for the next poor sod who dared to walk down the driveway.

'Is it wrong to admit I quite liked feeling a bit like a rockstar with all the cameras pointed at me?' Amelia asked. 'Hang on, isn't that Polly? I thought she was being calmed by a victim support person?'

'So did I, and yes, it is Polly.'

'Morning, Jamieson and whoever you are – I never did catch your name but I have no desire to know it either.'

Amelia's stare back could cut glass.

'Not the best of mornings, is it? Poor Jordan. Oh. well, at least he had a good time in the sack before he got bombed. An experience you missed out on, Jamieson. Your loss, Jordan's gain.'

'That's questionable.' Amelia couldn't help herself. 'It takes more than a can of cream and a few props to be good in the sack, and quite frankly, honey, I'm sure Jordan Sticks would have had better. Classier, to say the least.'

As Polly stalked off we turned into the main lane and I said to Amelia, 'You know she's a barrister? Quite a good one, I suspect.'

'Doesn't matter one jot to me.'

'I never thought it would.'

'Look at those daisies. Aren't they magnificent? I just can't get mine to grow like that at home yet they flourish here. Perfect weather for them.'

We looked across to the stream which was barely moving now due to lack of rain. Ducklings were toppling down the bank and seemed to enjoy their splash on landing. We walked into Bert's coffee shop.

'Jamieson, Amelia, good morning!' Bert shuffled out from behind the counter to greet us. 'What's going on at The Pied? No one down here's been told anything but the online papers are talking about Jordan Sticks being attacked and someone else dying! We're all worried, and I saw those thugs running away. It's madness. I thought the London tourists were the worst thing around here but murder trumps them.'

'Yes, well, Jordan Sticks was attacked. I may as well tell you now since you'll find out soon enough – it appears it was by some kind of explosive device.'

'You're kidding me?'

'Nope.'

'Wowsers. What did Jordan do to anyone apart from play outstanding soccer? Is he okay?'

'Last I saw him he was alive.'

'Bloody heck. What about the other person who was carried out in a body bag?'

'That was the uncle of the bride. He had a heart attack.'

'That's all? Just a heart attack – nothing sinister?'

'Yes.' Amelia responded so quickly I could tell she was in doubt.

Bert looked to the door. 'What are you doing in my shop? You're not welcome here. Trying to steal my fudge recipe?'

'Be quiet Bert.' It was Anne. 'I've come in to ask Jamieson and Amelia what's going on at The Pied. Not even the early tourists can get car parks. Everyone knows you're only selling supermarket fudge anyway – no competition for my homemade delight.'

'It's not supermarket fudge.' Bert went back behind the counter and pushed some empty packets into the bin. 'Coffee for both of you?'

'Yes, please.'

We explained to Anne what we had told Bert while he crashed and banged everything in sight in protest at Anne being in his shop.

'Bert, did you say you saw some thugs, as you called them, running through the village?' I asked.

'As a matter of fact, yes. I couldn't sleep a wink because I was so worried I'd left the coffee machine on, so I came down here at about 5:30am to check on it.'

'Left it long enough, didn't you?' Anne asked. 'You could have burnt down all our shops by then.'

'Be quiet or leave my shop! Anyway, I was nearly bowled down by those thugs. I assumed they had been up to no good – graffitiing or the likes. I'm surprised the cops haven't been in here asking me questions. There's no way I'm going to battle my way through that field of paparazzi to get to them.'

'I wouldn't have thought anyone would be interested in taking a photo of your old mug, Bert,' said Anne.

Thankfully the coffee was ready. 'Thanks, Bert. See you next time.'

As Amelia and I left, two police officers entered Bert's coffee house.

'That should give the old guy plenty to dine out on later.' Amelia sipped her coffee. 'This really is awful.'

'The worst. But it's caffeine and right now I need it.'

'Who do you think those thugs were?'

'I have no idea, but I'd say the police will be after them and the whole matter will be put to rest and we can go home.'

'Do you think Norrie died of a heart attack?'

'I hope so.'

My phone rang. It was Sandra so I walked over by the stream to talk.

'Jamieson, I have bad news. I couldn't get hold of the other shareholder – it was one major shareholder, a Singaporean company. The details are sketchy – I felt like I was on a goose chase trying to figure out who it was.'

'Who the hell would that be?'

'I don't know but it no longer matters because Sinclair has called me to say he is watching our shares being traded – it appears the large obscure shareholder is now selling and Frank D'Arcy and Corrin Smales have a new mate who's buying in at nine dollars. I don't want to be in business with those rats.'

'Who the hell is that? Okay, I have a plan. I'll get back to you.'

I called my contact at the *Financial Review*. 'Kyoko, I always like you to be the first person to know my moves.'

'You're a bad liar, Jamieson.'

'I have been in talks with Sandra to step down from Glasward-Sade Hart and start my own investment company.' That was factually correct. I just didn't mention the timing and the subsequent conversations with Sandra.

'Whoa, that is big news – straight off the back of a listing too.'

'It's a good opportunity for Glasward-Sade Hart – fresh blood and new investment ideas could make it even more profitable.'

'You know that's bullshit. You also know the commerce commission needs to hear things like that, given the timing of this call.'

'If the share price crashes I'm hurt too since I am an owner and potential seller of shares.

'I don't know what this is all about but there's no way I'm not running the story.'

I then called Sinclair. 'I suspect a whole lot of Glasward-Sade Hart shares are going to hit the market soon. Buy every single one for me, please.'

'Sure thing. What's going on?'

'I'll get back to you.'

I rang Sandra. 'Expect a call from Frank D'Arcy. The bastard will be asking you if it's true we've been in talks about me leaving the firm – say, "Yes, we have discussed it".' Still no lies.

Word travels fast when a financial reporter does a good job and, after a short time, I watched the market on my screen showing the price falling like a ton of bricks. D'Arcy, Smales and their mate weren't interested in the firm without me – I had stolen the revenge play of sacking me that they'd been paying for. They were like rats jumping from a sinking ship. They didn't know there was a shark circling in the waters below.

I called Sinclair, who said, 'Bloody heck, have you seen what's happened?'

'Yes. Have Frank D'Arcy and Corrin Smales and whoever else it is totally sold yet?'

'Yes, it's just come through – they got out at two dollars a share. They'd bought in at an average of eight so they've lost three-quarters of their money. Congratulations, Jamieson. You just sold fifteen percent of your firm at an average of seven-dollars-fifty a share and bought back thirty percent at an average of two dollars a share. A tidy profit.'

Sandra was calling. 'What the hell just happened there?'

'I believe I am now the majority shareholder of the firm,' I said happily.

'Bloody hell. I feel like I've been spun through a washing machine.'

'Should we discuss the repositioning of our names on the wall?'

'Very funny. I am still the managing partner.'

'And I'm fine with that. You might want to send out an email assuring all our clients that Glasward-Sade Hart is stable with no staff movements expected to occur – unless Jordan Sticks' attacker comes after me.'

'You're at the same hotel?'

'Yep. Fraid so.'

'Oh gosh, take care, although I'd say a famous soccer player has a greater chance of being attacked by a lunatic fan than a fund manager would.'

'Very funny, Sandra.'

The phone rang again – Sinclair. 'I have never had an irater phone call in my life.'

'Let me guess, from Frank D'Arcy?'

'He's talking legal action.'

'Tell him to knock himself out. I suggest he cuts his losses now though. Who was the third partner in their toxic trio?'

'Mario Sanchez.'

'You're kidding me?'

'No.'

'He's out of jail then?'

'Yes, and he was looking for ways to spend a ridiculous inheritance. It appears he hasn't forgiven you for the hostile takeover.'

'Seems I have an even bigger bounty on my back now with these guys.'

'You just hit them where it hurts – in the pocket – and they can't do much without any cash so I'd say you can sleep well at nights. Bastards deserved what they got today.'

'Thanks, Sinclair. I don't mind screwing people who are trying to screw me.'

'Is that a rooster? Where the hell are you?'

'In a village in the Cotswolds. Amelia and I are both here to witness friends renew their marriage vows. The problem is Jordan Sticks was one of the guests.'

'Whoa, I've been reading about that when not involved in your share trades today. A bomb – really?'

'Yes.'

'And another guy murdered?'

'No, that's media spin. It's unknown yet what happened to Norrie but I'm assuming – or rather hoping – it was a heart attack.'

Chapter 19

I found Amelia on the main lane, shopping bags in hand.

'The boutiques here are amazing. Not obvious from the street – all little hidden gems. No wonder the Londoners like coming here. Productive phone call, was it?'

'You could call it that. I am now the majority shareholder in Glasward-Sade Hart.'

'What? How did that happen? You know, don't worry, tell me another time, but congratulations.' Amelia hugged me and I did not want to let her go.

We walked together back to The Pied. The paparazzi were clearly making provisions for camping the night at the end of the driveway.

A reporter shoved a microphone in our faces. 'We've heard that Jordan Sticks is conscious and is expected to make a full recovery. It is unlikely though that he'll be able to play soccer for long time. Do you have any comment?'

'Nope.'

We arrived at the pub in The Pied to find Fraser and Sam seated at the same table. Inebriated. 'Long day, boys?'

'Cripes,' Fraser said, looking at his watch. 'Where did the time go?'

Veda approached, 'Jamieson, you're a smart guy. Can you help us with an argument we're having? A wind farm is going to be built about one hundred miles from here and I think it's a grand idea – clean, renewable power.'

'But the windmills will look like warts on the landscape,' Barbara objected.

'I really can't do this right now. Sorry, ladies. There's a Bacardi on the bar with my name on it. At least there's about to be.'

I walked over to Juliette, who said, 'You look like you need a drink.'

'Bacardi and Coke, please, with plenty of Bacardi.'

'No problems. I just had to call a regular dinner guest of ours and cancel his reservation for tonight. Not that he wanted to come after the village rumour mill started up. Funny guy, he's single and always brings his dates here. He and I have a code: if the date's going well he orders beef, which tells me to let the kitchen know to take their time; if he orders chicken the date isn't going well and he wants the meals out as fast as possible to end the evening sooner. Anyway, as I said, a death and an attempted murder at the hotel is turning people off – not surprising really.'

She passed me my drink. 'This is not quite what Clarence and I dreamed of when we left our London jobs. Hopefully the police will get to the bottom of it soon. I've never seen Clarence so stressed. Look at him, sitting over there with his computer, estimating the losses we'll incur with the lack of patronage. It's the pub that makes the money, not the bed and breakfast, and normally The Pied is pumping at nights – weekends in particular.'

She sighed. 'I love it out here in the country but I do miss London, you know. I told myself we'd be safer here than in the city, but now I feel like I have to watch my back. I know that's irrational – I know it was probably a mad fan who got Jordan Sticks and that Norrie had a heart attack, but, what if that wasn't the case for either of them? I don't feel quite so safe anymore.'

She looked sad. 'I knew Jordan Sticks before he became famous – met him through Tilda. He hung around her like a little brother. Always up to no good, cruising the streets, bouncing a soccer ball off some part of his body. I guess that's what made him so good at the sport. Clarence knew him too, although a little too well – he and Jordan had a run-in years ago when Jordan treated his sister badly. Well, that's what Clarence said – to me it sounded like a standard break-up. Still, men can be very protective of their sisters.'

Absently she wiped the bar. 'That all seems so long ago now. Jordan went on to become a famous soccer player, and Clarence an investment banker. Clarence was good, you know. Always seemed to be involved in the right deal at the right times – earnt enough money for us to do this.' She gestured around her. 'Sometimes he had to be very secretive though in case news got leaked to the media and a deal was sabotaged. I found that hard at the time, couldn't understand why he didn't trust me – now I realise he was just trying to protect me from having to think carefully about what I said to anyone. Am I pleased those days are gone! I was head of investor relations for British Gas. It paid the bills but I wanted more in life. As I said, as soon as the police and cameras leave the better, and then Clarence and I can return to normal.'

Donald Crabshaw, looking very happy, pulled up a stool at the bar. 'Your finest pinot noir, please Juliette.'

'You're the only person in this place who's looking upbeat,' Juliette commented.

'No point in being down, is there? I mean, Jordan Sticks will live to see another day and poor old Norrie wasn't really a surprise, was he?'

'Jordan's soccer career may suffer a bit though,' I suggested. 'When I saw him being lifted onto the stretcher he didn't look like he was in any state to make the big game he's got coming up.'

'Them's the breaks though, I guess, in competitive sport.' Donald loosened his tie. 'I'm sure he'll be back on the field soon enough.'

'Do you follow soccer?' I asked.

'Indirectly, you might say. I don't watch most games but I read the papers and I'm always aware of the scores, top players, things like that. Now that I have a minute with you I wanted to ask if you had any insight on the foreign exchange market? I'm looking to transfer a significant number of pounds to an offshore account. Do you have any ideas on where best to put it with the most favourable exchange rate and lowest taxes?'

'That's not really my area of expertise, sorry.' I sensed Donald Crabshaw was trying to pull off some dodgy tax-avoidance strategy and I wasn't going to give him advice on how to execute it.

'Shame. Oh well, I'm sure I'll figure something out. I'm looking for new opportunities – have had a bad run of things lately but it appears my luck may be turning.'

'Thank goodness for that!' Juliette blushed. 'Sorry to interrupt but I couldn't help overhearing. We like you, Donald, but you've had us pretty stressed for a while now.'

'It's always darkest before the dawn, Juliette, and in investing it's important to hold on for the long-term ride even if things get a little bumpy along the way. Panic never helped anyone.'

I was pleased Donald's performance appeared to be on the up – four years of a poor track record was enough to send any fund manager to the brink.

Donald continued, 'Did I hear you saying you knew Jordan Sticks when he was younger?'

'Yes,' replied Juliette. 'He always had so much enthusiasm for life. Got himself in trouble though, which was surprising – normally the sporty kids have less time on their hands for mucking about. Still, he did okay in the end, didn't he?'

'To say the least,' Donald replied. 'I am very happy, as I'm sure we all are, that he'll make it through this morning's event. If the online papers are correct, Jordan will be fine in a few months.'

'A few months makes a big difference to an athlete at that level in sport,' I noted. 'He'll miss the whole season.'

'Happens, doesn't it?'

'No, Donald, actually it doesn't just happen,' Juliette snapped. 'Sportspeople don't just happen to activate bombs when they open their hotel door. It is so horrific, and to think it took place here at The Pied.'

'Give yourself a break, Juliette.' Donald responded. 'There's nothing you could have done to protect Jordan from a mad fan. It's Norrie I'd be more concerned about.'

'Why?'

'Well, who knows how he actually died?'

'Donald, you are quite intolerable sometimes.' Juliette started frantically polishing glasses.

'Good evening all.'

I was startled to see Polly.

'Jamieson, you must introduce me to this man.'

Juliette had it wrong – it was Polly who was intolerable. Donald clearly thought he was above Polly and rudely left to go and sit by himself.

'Who does he think he is? Too good for everyone else? If he'd seen me in that sabotage case I won he might not be thinking that. Prize pillock.'

Judging by Donald Crabshaw's hunched shoulders he'd clearly heard her and didn't like being called a pillock.

'I've had enough, Barbara.' Veda raised her voice and pushed her chair back to leave, catching the eye of everyone in the room. 'You have got to stop thinking that we all operate like the royal family. It's delusional. This is real life, not some fantasy world that you operate in.'

'Shush, Veda, you're making a scene.' Barbara squirmed in her chair.

'Who cares? Why don't you liberate yourself for once and let other people's opinions just be? Why are you so bothered in keeping up appearances? It must be so tiring.'

'There is no need to air our dirty laundry in public. Stiff upper lip and all that.'

'I'm going for a walk.' Veda stormed out.

I re-joined Sam and Fraser. 'When do you think the police will let us go?' I asked Fraser.

'I don't know. It's tricky – we're officially still suspects, so they can't really afford to let us leave the country.'

'Poker, anyone?' Sam asked.

'Deal me in.'

Chapter 20

Next morning, I was woken by the cow Donald Crabshaw had taken exception to, so I put on my gear and headed out for a run. I was still mulling over who the initial large investor was in Glasward-Sade Hart. They had bought quickly, then sold to D'Arcy and the other rats – and made a good profit on it, no doubt.

The sky was full of clouds that had arranged themselves into various shapes. I jogged out to the west, a path I hadn't taken before – keen to see what else this part of the world had to offer.

A swingers' retreat. At least that's what it looked like from my position at the brow of the hill.

Veda walked past me. 'Hi, Jamieson. Care to come join us? It's a local nudist gathering. Everything is so much clearer nude, in nature.'

Ironically the group was in a small valley surrounded by hills – they seemed to want some privacy. I wondered if the paparazzi camped out at The Pied knew about this.

Veda took off her top as she walked down the hill and was fondly greeted by participants. A few pod-like tents were dotted around the valley and I could see horizontal movement in one.

Suddenly feeling like a pervert, I averted my gaze and continued my run, chuckling at the thought of what Barbara would say if she knew about this part of Veda's life. I also felt very aware of my own situational lack of female company and was determined to fix the drought when I returned to South Beach.

I was stopped in my tracks by my phone. It was Kenneth Chow. 'Jamieson, you seem to have a way of bringing me good luck.'

'How's that?' I asked, realising I was puffing hard – too much Bacardi last night?

Kenneth chuckled. 'You haven't figured it out yet, have you?'

I felt stupid. 'It was you, wasn't it?'

'That's right. When I heard you were listing Glasward-Sade Hart I wanted in on it. Seems I think you're a good bet. The strange thing was, I bought a significant number of shares after listing at seven-dollars-fifty each, then saw some other monkeys enter the market wanting to buy at nine. Too easy! I made a dollar fifty per share on all of them. I'll always back you, Jamieson, but I couldn't walk away from that trade.'

'Kenneth Chow, you old fox. You sold them at nine and I bought them back at two.'

'Huh?'

'Turns out the guys who were buying only wanted to make life very difficult for me by getting on the board and stuffing me around. On hearing the news that I could be leaving they wanted out. I suspect I know the one who choked first.'

'And you bought your own company back below what you sold it for?'

'That's right.'

Kenneth chuckled. 'Too good, Jamieson, too good.'

'I think everyone involved got what they deserved.'

'And we're still on for Xtrapak, are we?'

'Yes. I'm about to make another enemy there when we give marching orders to the CEO and most of the board.'

'They don't get any sympathy from me. The people who work hard in life deserve sympathy, not the free-riders who do nothing and expect to be paid millions a year. That CEO will get his legal payout which will set him up nicely for the rest of his life, I'd say.'

'I just need to convince him to sell.'

'Hopefully you are persuasive.'

'I'll call Sinclair and see what he can arrange. I don't need to do this face to face with Wes.'

'Yes, never make it personal.' Kenneth said goodbye.

So it was him. The man was a Singaporean billionaire for a reason – his ability to act on short-term opportunities was astounding.

I walked across the grass to the main lane and saw Bert, who was just opening the shop.

'Morning, Jamieson. I'm pleased you're still buying coffee – all the tourists have been scared off. This business had better be sorted soon. I'm losing money.'

'Don't the paparazzi drink coffee?'

'Not from here. They bring it in flasks from home – too worried about missing a photo opportunity to leave their spot. They've taken up all the car spaces too so even if a tourist did come to town they wouldn't be able to get a park.'

'Ah, those Londoners don't seem so bad now, do they?'

'I hate to say it but no. Look, I know I get my back up about them, but I guess at the end of the day they do pay the bills. I'm making a loss on this fudge though – it's got a very short expiry date and it's going off before I can sell enough of it.'

I looked at the fudge, still partially in plastic supermarket wrap with a sign *Homemade* in front of it. 'Bert, you're good at making coffee,' I lied, 'but maybe it's time to leave the fudge to Anne and focus on what you've been doing for years?'

'You may be right. Can I interest you in a piece with your coffee? Before it expires? This lot won't be replaced, I can tell you that.'

Reluctantly I said yes, took one bite as I left the shop, then threw the remainder in the bin around the corner.

As I approached the driveway to The Pied, I could see the paparazzi were desperately jostling for the best position behind the taped line Clarence had obviously installed.

'Sir, sir, we've heard another person has been attacked at The Pied. What do you know?' Microphones were pushed in my face while cameras clicked.

'I have no idea.' My first thought was for Amelia, then Fraser, Sam and Tilda. I ran along the gravel to the entrance of The Pied, then exhaled deeply and put my hands on my head when I saw Amelia. She was okay.

'Jamieson! I want out of here!' Amelia was crying. 'Polly has been found dead – shoved in a bush of daisies.'

'Polly? What the hell is going on?' The confusion was overwhelming.

Fraser turned from the police he'd been speaking to and walked towards me.

'Fraser, what's happening?'

'I'd like to know that myself. It seems Samrina found Polly – she saw some legs hanging out of the daisy bush over there and went to have a look. Got the fright of her life, I'd say.'

'Who did it? And how?'

'Who? I don't have a clue, but how? I do know that – she was stabbed.'

'Oh, my goodness!' Amelia shrieked. 'What's this all about? Who's going to be next?'

'That's what I want to know.' It was Samrina. 'I wasn't kidding when I asked at the picnic whether Norrie had really died of a heart attack. Then Jordan Sticks got attacked and now Polly. She wasn't even part of our group. Who was she?'

'She was a barrister from London who'd come here to escape the rat race and find some peace and quiet,' I said.

'Looks like she found peace.' Fraser's humour never had good timing. We all looked over to see Polly's red shoes sticking out from under the daisy bush. 'Clearly it was a rushed job,' Fraser continued. 'Personally, I would have removed the red shoes – made the hiding spot a bit less obvious.'

'How can you joke at a time like this?' Samrina bellowed.

'Come now, Samrina. Everyone has different ways of dealing with shocking situations.' Sanjay sounded very wise and remarkably tolerant. Even I thought my friend had crossed a humour line this time.

'What did Polly do to anyone?' Samrina asked.

'She did Jamieson.'

'Cheers, Amelia.'

'And she did Jordan Sticks.'

'She certainly didn't do me.' It was Donald Crabshaw, 'Odd girl – didn't know how to dress like a woman.'

'What the heck are you talking about, Donald?' Samrina demanded.

'Well, you know – she didn't wear skirts and dresses like a woman should. She was always in trousers or running gear. No man would be attracted to a girl in trousers.'

'Speak for yourself, Donald.' Sanjay's tolerance had obviously run out. 'I'm sick of you and your prejudice. It's about time you curbed that poisonous tongue of yours and figured out how to stop losing other people's money.'

'Defending Polly, are you? Did you do a few rounds with the woman as well, Sanjay?'

Sanjay punched him hard. Donald Crabshaw hit the gravel.

'About bloody time someone did that.' Barbara bustled over to take pleasure in Donald scrambling to get up off the ground, hand to his lip which was bleeding. 'You've got a strong character, boy. Why on earth did you marry a woman like her?' Barbara looked at Samrina, whose dark-brown eyes were steely.

'Barbara, leave them alone.' Veda had missed a button on her shirt, and was that a blade of grass in her hair?

'Where have you been, Veda? You silly woman, you've been missing during this whole Polly business. I hope the police don't suspect you. The shame you would put on the family. Oh, for goodness' sake, let's tell everyone who you really are. Margaret.

Everyone, Veda is Margaret – she changed her name years ago when she went alternative. Ridiculous, if you ask me. I will only ever now call you Margaret.'

'And I will only answer to Veda.'

I noticed she'd dodged telling Barbara her earlier whereabouts.

Sam and Tilda joined the group.

'What the hell?' Sam asked.

'This is the worst wedding ever,' Tilda sobbed.

'Vow renewal, honey – remember you made us all call it that?' Samrina folded her arms across her chest.

Clarence came over. 'Can everyone please come inside? We're making quite a scene out here.' He pointed to the multitude of camera lenses at the base of the driveway.

'Here we go again,' said Fraser as we headed into the pub for a further round of police interrogation.

Chapter 21

Detective Sergeant Bill took the floor. 'Right, we are now investigating the attempted murder of Jordan Sticks and the murder of Polly Barnes.'

'And Norrie?' Samrina asked.

'We are still awaiting the autopsy results. Samrina, we will start with you. Where were you at 9am this morning?'

'Sanjay and I were still in bed. We had stayed up late talking, planning our future, and time got away on us. We didn't wake until 9:15 – I know because as soon as I opened my eyes I saw my bedside clock.'

'That's right,' Sanjay replied. 'For once I woke feeling good. Can't say I feel the same way now.'

'And how do you two know Jordan Sticks and Polly Barnes?'

'We met Jordan Sticks through several of Donald Crabshaw's investment update meetings. They used to get quite heated and for some reason or another Jordan always seemed to back Donald. I guess he had relatively less to lose than the rest of us,' Sanjay said. 'As for Polly, I had never met her until we arrived at The Pied.'

'Jamieson knows Polly.'

'Shut up, Donald.' I'd had enough.

'Jamison, how is it you knew Polly Barnes?' Bill asked.

'We met when we were out for a run one morning.'

'Did you have sexual intercourse with Miss Barnes?'

'I'd like to think of it as a bit more fun than that, but yes.'

'I thought you had better taste than that. Actually, no – she's your ex-wife, isn't she?' Donald Crabshaw pointed at Amelia.

I'd had enough and stood to finish off what Sanjay had started outside.

'Sit down, please.' Detective Bill said.

'Donald's a twat.' I whispered to Amelia.

'I know,' she replied.

'And how did you know Jordan Sticks?' Bill was still looking at me.

'I first met him when Tilda introduced us here. I knew he was a soccer player though. I was out for a run at the time Polly was murdered. Veda can attest to that.'

Veda's eyes hit the floor.

'And you, Amelia?'

'I met the insecure dick in the pinstripes when I first arrived.'

'We are not interested in that. How did you know Polly Barnes and Jordan Sticks?'

'I met them both when I got here. I had a few chats with Jordan – who wouldn't? He's hot, let's be honest. Polly I encountered in Jamieson's room, and this morning I was with Tilda having a drink when Polly died.'

'Yes, she was,' Tilda agreed.

'There's the one you're looking for,' Donald boomed. 'Ex-wife catches ex-husband and lover in bed together. Then the temptress gets murdered. Take her to the station now.'

'Donald, I swear —'

'It's okay, Jamieson. Mr Crabshaw, I request you keep your mouth shut unless answering a direct question.'

'Oh, my goodness,' Amelia again whispered to me. 'I'm not looking so good, am I?'

I put my hand on her knee. 'Don't give it another thought.'

'Donald Crabshaw, how did you know Jordan and Polly?'

'Jordan was a client, a good one — not a whinger like the rest of the people here. Polly? She was just a bit of common catch, wasn't she? Never seen her before in my life. I was working all morning when she died.'

'Frittering away our money?' Veda asked. 'I've given you a lot of space, Donald, losing all that money of ours. Thought I'd give you the benefit of the doubt, but the way you've been talking about Polly Barnes is disgraceful. You should be ashamed of yourself.'

'I actually agree with you, Margaret,' Barbara said. 'The woman seemed fairly harmless, if a bit horny.' That word sounded odd coming from Barbara.

'And how do you know Jordan and Polly, Veda?'

'Same as Samrina and Sanjay. I met Jordan at Donald's client functions. Polly, I met her when I arrived here.'

'And where were you this morning?'

Veda knew I knew. 'At the swingers' valley.'

'Excuse me?' Bill said.

'What did you just say?' asked Barbara.

'I was with the swingers in the valley. I was swinging with a couple from Berkshire.'

'She's gone mad! Get help – my sister's having a turn!' cried Barbara.

'No, Barbara, this is me. I am a swinger and I like organic food and I believe in yoga and meditation and I run wellness retreats.'

'There are no swingers in my family,' Barbara turned her back on Veda.

'And you, Barbara?' Detective Bill asked.

'I went out for a walk across the meadow this morning, and had a conversation with one of the wonderful men trying to spot a rare blue thrush. Total gentleman. I knew Jordan Sticks from Donald's client meetings but I only met Polly when I arrived here. There. Done.'

'Clarence and Juliette?'

'We were busy getting The Pied ready for the day – not that we'll have any visitors with this publicity nightmare.' Clarence glared through the window, down the drive to the waiting paparazzi. 'Juliette and I both knew Jordan Sticks from Donald's client meetings and Polly had been a regular guest at The

Pied. She stayed here whenever she needed to get away from London.'

'You'd better tell them Clarence,' Juliette said. 'They'll find out anyway.'

'Very well, and I had a fling with Polly when I was working as a banker in London. She and I were both involved in the same deal. I cheated on Juliette, who did absolutely nothing to deserve it, and I regret it to this day.'

Samrina's mouth dropped open. 'Yet you let her stay at The Pied?'

'I knew Clarence would never do it again and I was more than happy to take money off the cow,' Juliette responded. 'She could waste her time flirting with Clarry – it was never going to go anywhere.'

'You're a bit too confident about that.' Donald Crabshaw laughed.

'Donald, back off,' Clarence shouted.

I don't think Donald had a friend in the room.

'And you, Sam?'

'I was in bed. Tilda had gone off with Amelia and I was watching the tennis on TV.'

'Who won?' I asked.

'Djokovic – he's facing Tsonga next.'

'And how did you know Mr Sticks and Miss Barnes?' Bill was getting frustrated.

'I met them when I arrived here.'

'Tilda?'

'I was the one who organised this whole, stupid affair.'

'Go easy on yourself, Tils,' Amelia soothed.

'Jordan was my next-door neighbour when I was younger – he's like a brother to me. I was able to talk to him by phone this morning. He sounded okay, thankful to be alive really, although annoyed to be missing the season. I don't know who could have done this.'

'And Polly?'

'I met her after we arrived at The Pied. It annoyed me when I saw her latching onto Jordan.

Jamieson can look after himself but Jordan was too sweet for the likes of Polly.'

It was hard to know which way to take that.

'And Fraser?' Bill asked. 'I know you're a detective in South Beach but I'd better include you in this for completeness.'

'Sure. I was in bed this morning – no point getting up ready to face more of this drama.' Fraser crossed his arms and leant back in his chair. 'And I only met Jordan and Polly when I arrived here.'

'Why aren't you asking everyone about Norrie?' Samrina asked again.

'As I said, we don't have the autopsy result back, so we do not yet know his cause of death. I won't investigate unless it is a confirmed murder case.'

'Isn't it obvious?' Samrina was frustrated.

Chapter 22

My phone rang. Mirabelle. I turned to Amelia, 'Have you already told your parents that Polly was murdered?'

'I've been texting them while we we're sitting here.'

'Have they got some kind of direct line to Mirabelle?'

'I think she pounces on them each time they leave the house and I know they were heading out for a walk.'

My phone stopped ringing. Phew. Then it started again. I should have expected it.

'Right, everyone. Once again, you are not to leave Avon-On -The-Water until we have furthered our investigations.' Bill headed to the door, and I answered my phone the third time it rang.

'Mr Hart, it is I –'

'Yes, Mirabelle. How are you?'

'I worried, I so worried, Mr Hart. Another murder. Thank you for being good boss. I hope I find other boss like you. Maybe I work for Mrs Hart when you dead.'

'Mrs Hart is here with me. It is interesting you think she will be coming home and not me.'

'Mrs Hart, she nice lady. No one murder Mrs Hart.'

'Okay, Mirabelle, thank you, I think, for your call but I assure you I will be home. Is that Rodrigo I hear in the background?'

'Yes, he has soap bubbles in spa bath. He have good time.'

I gagged and coughed and clenched a fist. Why did I ever agree to this before I'd left South Beach? I had been distracted by a work deal. Never again. I closed my phone.

'Trouble at home?' Amelia grinned.

'I'm going to fire that woman.'

'No, you're not.'

She was right. If I fired Mirabelle I would have to do my own washing and that wasn't gonna happen.

'Do you think the police are onto the guys Bert heard running past his shop?'

'I'd say so. They're not the friendliest looking cops so I think I'd leave them to it.'

Fraser interrupted, 'The detective's okay, and yes, they're searching for the alleged thugs.'

'Excuse me, guys, I need to make a call.' I got up from my seat and walked outside to call Sinclair.

'No sheep, cows or roosters in the background this time?'

'No, they tend to get scared off by police and reporters. A woman was found dead in a daisy bush.'

'Huh? Sounds almost comical.'

'Nope, it is true, and I may be a prime suspect because I shagged her before she died and Amelia caught us.'

'What the hell?' I could imagine Sinclair's right eyebrow was near his hair-line at this point.

'Yeah, don't ask. Let's just say it wasn't one of my finer moves. Now, I need you to call Wes at Xtrapak and make an offer for me to buy his company. I will give him twenty-six million.'

'Whoa, where did this come from?'

'Kenneth Chow and I want to turn Xtrapak around and use the profits to make further investments – a Berkshire Hathaway for want of a better word. I'd prefer it if you didn't tell him Kenneth was involved – he knows a billionaire has deep pockets.'

'I'll see what I can do. So the whole convertible debt thing...?'

'Yesterday's business. But it has nothing to do with this deal since it went through Glasward-Sade

Hart Funds Management, not this new arm of the firm'

'Righto.'

Amelia was walking towards me, and even in this atmosphere she was striking. She'd tied her brunette hair back into a messy ponytail. Her legs went on forever. She was a forbidden temptress and sometimes drove me crazy.

'Want to go searching out a rare blue thrush?' She handed me a pair of binoculars.

'I didn't know you were into bird-watching?'

'I'm not but I'm too scared to sit around here – I don't want to be the next person murdered. And I'm fairly sure you're not the murderer so I figured I'd hang with you.'

'Why not?' I had nothing better to do myself.

'Hold up!' Fraser was running across the gravel towards us. 'Where are you two going?'

'To watch birds, it appears,' I replied.

'I love bird-watching.'

'No, you don't.'

'Suddenly I do. I would rather watch birds than hang about that lot.'

'You'd better get some binoculars,' Amelia suggested.

'My eyes will do just fine.'

'Guys. Wait!' This time it was Sam, with Tilda clutching his hand. He yelled at us, 'We're coming where you're going.'

On reaching us, Tilda said, 'I don't know what's going on at The Pied, but it's dawned on me I don't really know anyone there. I thought I did, but truthfully, I've been holding on to old relationships that have changed. I don't feel close to any of those people any more. Jordan is the only one I care about and he's okay – thank goodness. The rest of my supposed friends here feel more like strangers. I guess we all change as we get older, drift apart. I'm with you guys. What are we doing?'

'Bird-watching.'

'Hang round with a potential murderer or watch birds?' said Sam. 'I'm in – let's go find that feathered thing.'

We ambled across the grass towards a grouping of willows.

'Look up in these branches. Can anyone spot a bird?' Amelia was peering through her binoculars.

'I really don't give a toss,' Fraser said as he sat on the ground and started rubbing sticks together.

'I can't keep pretending either – a bird's a bird. Who do you think killed Polly?' Sam was talking to no one in particular.

'It's a bit hard to talk about this, Sam, when all the suspects are Tilda's friends.'

'Thanks, Amelia, but I'm fine. It has to be one of them – I just have no idea who.'

'What about Veda?' Sam said. 'Whose real name isn't even Veda, although I do vaguely remember being told that.'

'I saw her heading down to join the swingers,' I said. 'She's all right. There's something quite sexy about her, actually.'

'She's seventy!' Tilda said.

'I know. Still...'

'One thing that can be said about Jamieson is the man has range,' Amelia smiled. 'He started this trip with a twenty-something-year-old.'

I remembered why it's never a good idea for your ex-wife to mix with your current interests.

'Where are these swingers?' Fraser was interested.

'In the valley over there. You can't see it from here – it's beyond the brow of the hill.' I pointed.

'Anyone keen to have a look?' Fraser asked.

'Yeah, why not?' Sam started walking and the rest of us followed.

'Thank goodness the ground is dry and I can walk through the grass without sinking, unlike last time,' said Amelia. 'That's when I first met Donald Crabshaw, all proper and totally offended by the sight of me with my box of plasters.' Amelia pulled off a posh English accent remarkably well.

'I'm sure he wasn't as bad as that when we were younger,' said Tilda.

'I doubt Samrina and Sanjay have anything to do with the attacks.'

'Why do you seem so sure about that, Amelia?' Fraser asked.

'They're too nice really. Samrina's a management consultant, like I used to be – in fact sometimes I look at her and think she's the old me, only an Indian version. I like her.'

'Sometimes it's the most surprising people who are capable of terrible crimes,' Fraser replied. 'I'd say if it were one of them it would be Sanjay. I just get a funny feeling about him.'

'I think Samrina would have noticed if Sanjay was that way inclined,' Amelia pointed out. 'Besides, I disagree with you; I like Sanjay.'

'It's got to be Clarence, hasn't it?' said Sam. 'Maybe Polly was blackmailing him somehow. They did have a fling, and isn't it weird that Polly used to come and stay at The Pied a lot?'

'Polly's a bit wacky,' I told him.

'Oh, yes, that's right – of course you would know.' Tilda laughed. 'Do you like jam with your cream, Jamieson?'

Amelia had obviously been blabbing. I changed the topic. 'Wouldn't it be Juliette, in that case? Maybe she was sick of Polly being in her face?'

'No one has mentioned Barbara.' Amelia had finally stopped her side laugh with Tilda.

'I think that woman lives in some fantastical world where she believes she knows the royal family, or is part of it, or something. I don't think she's capable of functioning in normal society,' Fraser replied.

'Maybe that would make it easier for her to kill someone?' Amelia asked.

We came to the brow of the hill. 'There it is,' I said. Even more tents dotted the landscape, with sheep grazing around the swingers – it was a kind farmer who had offered their land for this purpose.

'You are kidding me. No way.' Sam started laughing. 'Look over there beside the green tent.' He pointed.

It was pinstripes.

'Donald, the old dog. Too good for common people – unless they're swinging,' I laughed.

'He must have heard about it from Veda,' Amelia suggested. 'Yuk, who would want to do it with him?'

'That's a bit harsh,' said Sam.

'No, it's not,' Tilda contradicted him.

Donald started stripping.

'I can't watch this.' Amelia covered her eyes but peeked through the slits between her fingers.

'Hey, you lot up there – want to come and join us?' We'd been spotted by one of the naked ones.

'Ah, I think that's our cue to leave.' Sam and Tilda started running like teenagers. As we walked off I noticed Donald quickly straightening his tie. He knew he'd been seen and I could imagine this wouldn't suit his public image.

'That was hilarious!' Sam laughed as we regrouped by the cow. 'Who would have thought?'

My phone rang, it was Sinclair.

Jamieson, I just got off the phone from Wes at Xtrapak. He wants twenty-eight million and to remain as CEO.'

'He's dreaming. Tell him he gets twenty-nine million and he issues a press release about retiring to spend more time with his family. He's got two months with the firm and then he's gone.'

'Okay, I'll give it a shot.'

Chapter 23

I needed a coffee. After checking no one else wanted one, I left the South Beach crew together and pushed through the crowd of reporters to visit Bert.

He was sitting on a stool outside his coffee shop. 'No customers. Place has been empty all morning. Have I mentioned how much I love the London tourists?'

A murder in the village had certainly changed Bert.

'The police just found those thugs, you know. They said my description was helpful. They're taking them to the station in Bardon to talk to the brutes. Hopefully they had something to do with the attacks and this whole business can be put to rest.'

The buzzer rang as Anne opened her shop door. 'Would you like a piece of fudge, Bert, Jamieson? Fresh this morning.'

'I'd be delighted.' Bert helped himself from the tray.

'I thought I'd see if I could sell any to the group of reporters since there's no one else to do business with around here apart from the odd passing local.'

'Your fudge is very good, you know, Anne,' said Bert.

'As is your coffee, Bert,' Anne lied as she walked on.

Bert got up off his stool. 'You're here for coffee, I guess?'

'Yes, please.'

'I will happily serve my one customer of the day.'

Coffee in hand, I returned to the driveway of The Pied. The paparazzi were becoming tiring. I skyped my Singapore work office.

'Jamieson, hellooooo.'

I had actually missed Penelope's drawl and was quite happy to hear a familiar voice.

'Any movements I should know about?' I asked.

'No, but performance is looking good. We're up four percentage points compared to the market. Kirk's celebrating with a chocolate doughnut. I don't know how he can eat food like that and still stay thin as a rake. How did the vow renewal ceremony go?'

'Not as expected. The bride's uncle died beforehand, someone tried to bomb the famous soccer player guest, and a woman – who seemed to have no links to the wedding party – was murdered.'

'Sandra told me you were with Jordan Sticks. Did you get his autograph or a selfie with him?'

'No.'

'Why not?'

'Not my style.'

'Jamieson –' Sandra's head appeared in the screen '– I need you in Singapore. We've got new clients knocking on our door. It seems any publicity is good publicity, and hearing about you potentially leaving us appears to have forced people who'd been thinking of investing to make the move to call us and find out what's going on.'

'Great news.' I was very aware that once Sandra had a potential client on the phone it was unlikely they would walk away. 'I will hopefully be allowed to leave here soon. I'll go home to say hi to the kids in South Beach then fly over.' I spend a lot of my life in the air.

Outside The Pied, all the wedding guests were seated at tables. The umbrellas were up and Juliette was busy hanging bunting flags on them. She was obviously trying to delude local passers-by that there was an air of joviality at the place.

'Where have you lot been?' Barbara demanded. 'I am too scared to walk anywhere alone now with a murderer about. Who are you people anyway? Where is South Beach? In one of the colonies? It's probably one of you lot who was responsible for these attacks, I doubt you have the same respect for life as we British do.'

'Where's a gun? There's about to be another murder,' Fraser whispered to me, staring at Barbara.

'Gees, I hope we can laugh about this over a beer at the tennis club when back home,' said Sam.

'Barbara, stop being so rude,' said Tilda. 'These are my friends you're insulting.'

'And we are your family. Blood is thicker than water, Tilda dear, you know that.'

'Actually, I don't think I do.' Tilda leaned back into the arms of Sam.

Amelia whispered to me, 'I think Sam and Tilda needed a murder around them to revive their relationship.'

I whispered back, 'Did it have the same effect on us?'

'Nope.'

I would continue to hold onto hope.

'So, what do we do now?' Sanjay asked.

'Sit like ducks and wait for the police to tell us we can leave this stupid place,' Samrina replied.

Detective Bill called Tilda over. She returned smiling.

'I have good news! Uncle Norrie had a heart attack. Oh no, that came out badly. The heart attack isn't good news but when the other option is murder, I'm happy.'

'Thank goodness,' said Samrina. 'I really thought he'd been done in. I guess that is somewhat settling.'

And so the absurdity of our time at The Pied continued, with everyone celebrating the fact that a man had suffered a heart attack.

'May my brother now rest in peace,' said Barbara. 'And it is good news that the Jordan Sticks boy is going to be okay. Who was this Polly woman and why would anyone murder her? Sounds like it's all a terrible coincidence if you ask me.'

'No one was asking you,' Veda replied.

'I'm still not going to be left alone with any non-South-Beacher,' Amelia said to me. 'One of those others is very likely guilty of murder and I don't want to be by myself finding out who it is.'

The timing of my phone ringing was bad. It was Sinclair. 'Are you okay if I take this?' I asked Amelia. She nodded and I walked away from the group for some privacy.

'Good news, Jamieson – Wes has taken the deal. He said he'd happily leave, and to tell you he would have accepted twenty-eight million.'

'Tell him I would have offered thirty.'

'I think I'll just let that go through to the keeper. Anyway, you now have your own investment company. We will need to talk later to sort through the details, but congratulations.'

After I'd hung up from Sinclair, I called Kenneth Chow. 'Kenneth, we are now officially invested together.'

'Excellent news. How much did we have to pay for Xtrapak?'

'Twenty-nine million.'

'A bargain. I sense this is going to work out very well, Jamieson. Remember, I am a silent investor. Good luck in shaking up the business.'

'Thanks, Kenneth. I'll be in touch.'

My first job would be to sack the board – replace the lazy baboons with people I respected.

Chapter 24

Amelia came over. 'Jamieson, Detective Bill wants us all inside the pub. I think he knows who did the attacks and he's going to reveal it to us in Poirot style. I hope he doesn't think it's me because I saw Polly in your room – I'm getting worried.'

'You're just being paranoid. It'll be fine.'

We walked into the pub and took the last two chairs in the circle Detective Bill had arranged.

'Thank you for coming, everyone,' Bill started.

'It's not like we had a choice,' Donald Crabshaw pointed out.

Bill ignored him. 'This was a difficult case. It was you, Juliette, who appeared to have the strongest motive. How could a woman be so calm in the face of her husband's ex-lover coming to visit so often? But Polly wasn't all she seemed, was she?'

'No.' Juliette dropped her head.

'We found regular payments from Clarence and your joint bank account into Polly's. I suspect her visits here were to lord her power over you?'

'Oh, gosh, she was awful!' Juliette put her head in her hands and started sobbing.

'Don't say anything, Juliette,' Clarence warned.

'It doesn't matter now – the police know.' Juliette turned to Bill. 'Polly was blackmailing us – well, Clarence really, but I love him, so when she came after him she came after me as well. She convinced us she had proof that Clarence traded on inside information on one of his deals as a banker. The penalty for that is a jail sentence. We chose to pay Polly instead.'

'I am so sorry Juliette, your life would have been very different if you hadn't met me and I hadn't had an affair with Polly. You don't deserve any of this mess.' Clarence's eyes teared up.

'The alleged insider trading is not part of this case so will not be dealt with here,' Bill stated.

'But it's clear they did it – lock them away,' Donald Crabshaw shouted.

Clarence put his arm around Juliette.

Bill continued, 'And you, Barbara…'

'Oh, dear me, I have nothing to do with any of this.'

'But you also knew Polly, didn't you? Yet you didn't tell us. She was your barrister when you were caught up in a dispute over a gambling debt, wasn't she?'

'Barbara?' Veda looked as surprised as the rest of us.

'I am not going to air my affairs in public, Detective Bill, so you can stop right there. I will not be humiliated.'

'How did you feel when you saw Polly here? Worried you would need to explain how you knew her? It can be fascinating how far a person will go to maintain their appearances.'

'He's right,' Fraser whispered to me.

'Barbara?' Veda looked to her sister.

'Oh, Veda, it all got so messed up.'

'It's okay, Barbara.' Veda hugged her. Sibling love ran deep despite everything.

'But I didn't kill Polly.' Barbara sobbed on Veda's jumper.

'No, you didn't,' Bill concurred.

'Was it Veda?' Donald Crabshaw asked.

'We couldn't find any connection between Veda and Polly.'

'Still, she harboured secret, dark tendencies and took her opportunities when they presented themselves.' Donald was no longer making sense and had started sweating.

'And you, Samrina and Sanjay.' Bill changed his focus. 'You also had no connection to Polly, whereas everyone in the room knew Jordan Sticks – or at least knew he was a famous soccer player.'

'It's too hot in here,' Donald panicked. 'Someone open a window!'

'Mr Crabshaw,' Bill addressed Donald. 'We were able to catch and question three young men seen running past Bert – the coffee shop owner – soon after the explosion that hurt Jordan Sticks. The men were very forthcoming during questioning. It seems they value their freedom. They identified you, Donald Crabshaw, as the person who paid them to plant the explosive device outside Jordan Stick's room. It was in the boot of your car – all they had to do was remove it, plant it outside the door, then run.'

Donald was stuck in a cage of eyes with no way out.

'Donald?' Tilda asked.

'It's all your fault!' Donald threw his hands up and looked at everyone. 'You couldn't accept that a fund manager can have bad performance. You had to come after me, attack me, remove your money from my business. You lot would have taken me to my knees if I hadn't done something.'

'Jordan didn't take his money from you,' Samrina protested.

'No, he was the only loyal one out of the lot of you.'

'So what did he do wrong?' Clarence asked. 'Why the heck did you feel the need to plant an explosive for him to trigger!'

'He played for Ramlock United.'

'Huh?' Juliette was stumped.

'Flipping heck,' I whispered to Fraser. 'I think I know where this is headed.'

'Sure you don't want to change your day job and become a detective?' Fraser asked me.

'Nope.'

Bill continued, 'Donald Crabshaw had shorted shares in Ramlock United. The attack on Jordan Sticks was an act of sabotage.'

'What does that mean – *shorted*?' Veda asked.

Detective Bill looked at me, 'Jamieson, you can probably explain this better than me.'

I faced Donald with disgust, and told the group, 'He would have borrowed Ramlock shares from another unsuspecting fund manager, sold them on the share market, then planned to buy them back at a far lower price than he'd paid for them when the share price got hit by the news that Ramlock's star player, Jordan Sticks, was out for the season. He would have then returned the shares to the lending fund manager and pocketed a nice profit.'

'Which would have all gone to you lot to keep you off my back.' Donald was on the attack. 'Relentless, all of you. You could drive a man to … to…'

'Murder?' Bill asked. 'Would you like to tell the room why you killed Polly Barnes?'

'I tried to get you too, Jamieson, just never found the opportunity. Then I figured if you knew something, you would have said, so I left you – you lucky bastard.'

'What the fuck are you talking about, Donald?'

'I heard you and Polly talking in the bar. She said the word *sabotage* and I thought she was on to me.'

'I remember you squirming, Donald, but I assumed it was because she'd just called you a pillock. Polly was talking about a sabotage case she'd recently won, not you sabotaging Jordan and Ramlock, you sack of …'

'That's enough,' said Bill. 'Donald Crabshaw, I am arresting you on the murder of Polly Barnes and the intent to cause grievous bodily harm to Jordan Sticks. You do not have to say anything, but it may harm your defence if you do not mention, when questioned, something which you later rely on in court. Anything you do or say may be given in evidence. Do you understand?'

Donald was handcuffed and taken out of the room.

Chapter 25

'Well, I never saw that coming,' Sam stretched.

'Jamieson understands how all this finance business works. He knew what was going on when Bill started talking,' said Fraser, 'It would have been helpful if you'd devoted time to figuring it all out earlier.'

'I had other things on my mind.'

'Is it time we all booked a flight back to South Beach?' Sam asked.

'Couldn't come soon enough,' said Fraser.

'Are you going via London?'

'Nope, not worth it. I want to go home.'

'I want to go to the hospital on the way to the airport,' said Tilda. 'I need to see Jordan before we leave.'

'Of course,' replied Sam.

'They didn't bring up the whole me seeing Polly in Jamieson's room business,' Amelia said. 'I was worried for a while there.'

'Seems detectives generally know what they're doing,' Fraser stood up for his fellow professionals.

'I'd better just go and say goodbye to the others.' Tilda approached Clarence and Juliette, who seemed relieved, but were obviously worried Clarence would be charged with insider trading.

Veda and Barbara were talking, which was a change from yelling.

Sanjay and Samrina walked past us. 'Nice meeting you,' Samrina said. 'Wish it was under better circumstances. We're going to pack our bags and drive back to London.'

My phone rang. Mirabelle. I couldn't bring myself to answer it. Amelia and her folks were ridiculously quick at communicating.

A text message appeared on my screen.

Mr Hart, it is I, Mirabelle. I know you are okay. You are alive and the murderer is caught. I so happy. I see you soon when you back home in South Beach. My Rodrigo, he cleaning spa pool.

It'd better be with bleach, but even so, the whole thing was being replaced.

The police car containing Donald Crabshaw parted the sea of photographers and reporters who jumped into their vans to follow.

'Want to go and call the kids?' Amelia asked.

'I sure do.'

We walked across the meadow and heard the church bells ring whilst the cicadas went about generating their merry tunes. The countryside was simply charming.

'There it is! In that willow!' Amelia startled me as she grabbed hold of my arm and pointed. I followed her finger and saw it.

A rare, blue thrush.

Other books in the Jamieson Hart series:

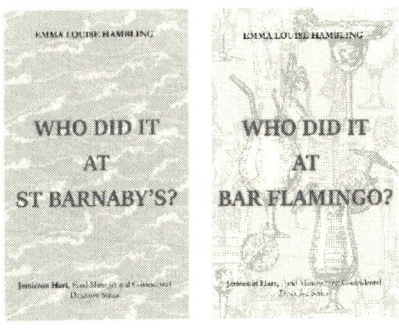

88305325R00143

Made in the USA
Columbia, SC
27 January 2018